A FREE STORY!

The Day We Met is a prequel short story
to the *Love on the Island* series.

***This short story is available FREE
only to members of my Readers' Group.***

Go to helenahalme.com to sign up to my
Readers' Group and get your free, exclusive, story now!

COPYRIGHT

AN ISLAND SUMMER

HELENA HALME

CHAPTER ONE

Andrei looks out of the bus window at the unfamiliar landscape. He knows from the map on his phone that they are somewhere in the middle of southern Sweden, on a two-lane motorway. He's just managed to snooze a little and feels groggy and wants to pee. But the light on the toilet is red, so he has to wait.

The journey from his small home village in Romania has taken three days and nights so far. He slept a little at the bus station in a city called Malmö, where he changed buses in the middle of the night, but he is still tired. His limbs are heavy and stiff from days of sitting in buses, with varying degrees of comfort – something that is improving the farther north he travels.

To distract himself, he takes out his phone and gazes at the last picture he took of his little brother. Smiling, the mop of his sand-colored hair falling over his eyes, and his hands on his hips, with the straps of his massive rucksack visible over his wide, flat chest, Daniel looked happy. He was standing outside the bus, on a sunny day, with his hands up, his fingers in a victory salute.

I should never have let him go.

Andrei swipes the image of his brother away and places his phone back in his pocket. He recalls the day, only two weeks ago, when he saw the policeman, old Grigore Levandovschi, drive his ancient motorcycle towards the barn. Andrei was showing his other brother, Mihai, how to use the new milking machine they'd just bought. Mihai is ten years younger than Andrei and was only five when their dad died. Their father had driven his bicycle into a ditch and hit his head on a stone. He'd been on his way back from the village where he spent the evenings downing shots of moonshine with his friends.

Andrei, the eldest of the brood of three boys and one girl, had to step in to help their mother.

'How has it taken nearly a year to let us know?' Andrei asked the policeman after he'd read the document. 'We have the internet, why didn't you just email me?' he added.

The policeman, a man in his seventies, well past his retirement age, just shrugged his shoulders. Andrei had known Grigore all his life, from when he was a little boy in shorts. When he was thirteen, the officer had arrested him for stealing cigarettes from the village shop. He'd brought Andrei home to face his mother, holding onto his ear, which really hurt. But it hurt more to see the disappointment in his mother's face.

'I wanted to bring you the sad news myself,' officer Levandovschi said in a response to Andrei's question.

His eyes were watery. He'd known Daniel too, since he was a baby.

Andrei didn't want to look up at the old man. He didn't want to start blubbering in front of officer Grigore.

'Thanks be to God your mother didn't have to live to suffer the loss of her child. Such a young age too,' the policeman sighed.

Andrei stood there while Grigore Levandovschi got on his motorcycle and, waving his hand, drove away. Dust billowed behind his back tire.

'What was that?' Mihai shouted from inside the barn. He was attaching the steel tubes onto the cow's udders – too loosely, no doubt.

'Nothing. Just concentrate on what you are doing,' Andrei said and put the piece of paper in the pocket of his overalls.

After dinner, which his sister Maria prepared for the three of them, Andrei went out for a walk. He wanted to make sure the cows were happy and that Mihai hadn't messed up the milking with the new machine. Leaning on the fence along the road, he gazed at the animals. His cattle looked happy enough, pulling at the dry grass, chewing loudly. Andrei lifted his eyes toward the dark, moonlit sky. If there was no rain soon, he'd have to buy expensive feed. It was August, and they still had the long fall to endure. What if it didn't rain until October? Perhaps it had been foolish to invest in new machinery after all?

But the future of the farm was nothing compared to the news the old policeman, Grigore, had brought him today.

Andrei pulled the envelope from the pocket of his overalls and looked at the text.

Daniel died nearly a year ago. Drowned in a fishing accident. That explained the lack of contact. It's what Andrei had suspected, but to read it on a piece of paper, black on white, was different. It was final.

Andrei gazed at the document again and saw the name of the investigating officer: Ebba Torstensson.

Later that evening, Andrei went to the little set of drawers in the kitchen and read through the letters from Daniel. He was looking for names.

He took out his cell and searched the web. Ebba Torstensson still worked for the police in Åland.

'The idyllic island of your dreams.'

That's what the Russian who'd sold Daniel the foolish idea to emigrate had called the place where his younger brother had gone.

Andrei wasn't interested in the Russian anymore. He knew how they operated; they will not give you anything but they will always take. And Andrei wasn't willing to give anymore. He wasn't sure what the police on this dreamy island were like – corrupt or not – so he will steer clear of Ebba Torstensson too. He will pay for information if he needs to, but he will start somewhere else. What he needs is the name of the girl.

CHAPTER TWO

Frida opens the door to Hilda's house with her own key, trying to do it as quietly as possible. It's just gone midnight, and she yawns as she enters the hall. There's a light coming from the lounge, which brings a smile to Frida's lips.

'I told you not to wait up,' she says and goes to hug Alicia.

'I was reading,' the older woman replies and adds, 'Did you have fun?'

Frida sits herself down opposite Alicia on a chintz-covered sofa. It has a straight back and is not the comfy kind that Frida has in her new home. Hilda, Alicia's mother, keeps the house sparklingly clean and tidy – as if she was expecting to host a photo shoot for an interior magazine. Frida can't compare it to her own home, which is always messy, to say the least.

'How was she, did she go down OK?'

Alicia smiles back at her.

'Anne Sofie was a dream, like always.'

Frida is aware this is probably a white lie, but she knows how much Hilda and Alicia dote on the girl. Lately, nearing her first birthday, her daughter has become very clingy. But Alicia had insisted Frida go out and enjoy herself.

Alicia leans toward Frida and asks again, 'So did you have fun?'

'Sure.'

'You don't sound so certain.'

Alicia's kind eyes are poised on Frida.

'You know, people get so drunk all the time.'

Alicia nods, 'Especially the tourists, they seem to come here just to get wasted. We just thought you ought to be with people of your own age. You spend far too much time with us oldies.'

'You're hardly old!' Frida protests, knowing that the woman smiling at her could easily be her mother, and Hilda her grandmother.

'You're too kind. But talking of wasted, I'm off to bed,' Alicia says. 'Hilda retired some time ago, but I would guess she's still up reading. If you see a light under her door, just pop your head in to say you're back. You know how she worries.'

'Of course,' Frida says and the two women hug.

'I'm very lucky to have you both,' Frida adds before opening the door for Alicia.

She watches as Alicia walks briskly over the yard to her own small house – an old milking parlor that was converted last year, after Alicia's stepdad died suddenly. Frida yawns once more and makes her way upstairs.

After she's said a quick hello to Hilda, kissed her

sleeping daughter goodnight, and settled into the attic room that Hilda has prepared for her, Frida is suddenly wide awake.

She knows both Alicia and Hilda mean well. They are the surprise extra family she gained after her boyfriend, Alicia's son, died suddenly. Even though Anne Sofie isn't Stefan's baby, the two women took her under their wing. They even call themselves granny and great grandma! And all this after she lied to them about who the baby's real father was.

Frida knows she couldn't have managed with the baby – or at least it would have been a lot more difficult – without their help. Yet sometimes she feels so incredibly lonely that her heart simply aches.

It aches for Stefan, but also for Daniel, Anne Sofie's real dad. She never loved him in that way, and the sex they'd had was more to do with their mutual sadness after Stefan's accident than any attraction. But he was a true friend. And she knows he would have been a good father.

Tears prick behind Frida's eyelids and she lets them well and fall onto her cheeks.

She has lost so many people, including her mother, who suffered from dementia for years. She'd spent the last eighteen months of her life in an old people's home and had slowly lost the grip on reality. Still, she was physically present, and when Frida visited every day, there were moments when she remembered her daughter. Frida's deep regret is that her mom didn't realize that the baby Frida was holding and showing her was her own granddaughter.

The next morning Alicia and Frida sit at the breakfast table nursing their cups of coffee while Anne Sofie sits in a wooden high chair, concentrating on eating a piece of rye bread. It's her favorite, and it never fails to amuse Alicia how the girl squeals when she sees her mother butter the top of the bread. Then, when Frida hands it over, Anne Sofie crams as much of it inside her mouth as possible, her whole baby body absorbed in the task.

'We need to do this more often so that you can get out a bit,' Alicia says, turning her face from the little girl toward Frida.

'Sure,' Frida replies.

But there's no conviction in her voice. Alicia gazes at the young woman. Motherhood suits her. She had a round face and a plump appearance when they first met, made more striking by the rainbow colors she used to sport – from her hair down to her Doc Martens, she'd wear every shade under the sun. She'd been pregnant, of course, but Alicia suspects, also carrying a little puppy fat. Now her hair is fair, its natural color, Frida supposes, framing her pretty blue eyes and small mouth. Although she still wears colorful clothes, the shades are more muted and stylish. Her slim body has a beautiful, feminine shape to it. Surely she'd have young men of her age queuing up to take her out?

Alicia places her hand over Frida's.

'You don't have to be alone forever, you know.'

'But I miss him so much,' Frida's eyes fill with tears.

Alicia's breath catches in her throat. The pain of losing her beautiful son, which she has now learned to control, rises, and she removes her hand and gets up. She walks to the kitchen counter.

'More coffee?' She asks Frida with her back to the girl.

Then she feels Frida's hand on her shoulder.

'I'm sorry, Alicia. That was very selfish of me.'

Alicia turns and forces her lips into a smile.

'No, it wasn't. We have to be able to talk about Stefan. But it's so hard...'

Frida puts her arms around Alicia and the two women stand still for a moment until there's a sharp cry from the table.

Frida goes over to Anne Sofie and picks up the piece of bread that has fallen on the ground.

'Oh dear, little girl. I'd better give you another one.'

The girl yelps again and kicks with her tiny chubby feet against the high chair.

'Patience, my baby,' Frida laughs.

Alicia too, smiles, relieved that they have changed the topic of conversation. She pours them both more coffee and returns the pot to the machine on the kitchen counter.

However much she'd like to, she still can't quite trust herself to reminisce about Stefan. Connie, her counsellor in London, whom she still telephones once a month, says she has to be patient.

'The day will come when you can remember the good times without pain.'

But Alicia can't imagine a situation where she doesn't feel utter sadness and when her chest doesn't contract at the mere mention of her son's name.

Grief can overwhelm her at the most unexpected moments. Only the other day, coming into the house, there'd been a strong smell of *Ålands pannkaka*, a clafoutis-type dessert typical to the islands. Hilda was making a batch for her bed and breakfast guests, a family staying in the red cottage. The *pannkaka* was an absolute favorite of Stefan's and Alicia could imagine her son sitting at the kitchen table, wolfing down a large portion of the dessert with Hilda's homemade plum jam.

A pain hit Alicia's lungs with such force, she had to sit down in the hall and wait until her breathing returned to normal. Luckily her mother hadn't heard her enter and Alicia was able to deal with the incident on her own. Hilda would only have made it worse with her fussing.

She can't remember Stefan without pain, which seems a betrayal somehow. This is something Alicia didn't tell Connie and doesn't plan to. The woman doesn't need to know everything.

CHAPTER THREE

After two days of traveling on uncomfortable buses, we stop in the middle of woods. It's dark and the Russians tell us to be quiet when they usher all of us off the bus. They're mostly young men like myself, from various parts of the country, all holding just one rucksack or bag. I nod to the only couple, a young girl and what I imagine is her brother, but they are not in the mood for talking. The girl has two long braids either side of her head and her eyes are large. Is she frightened? I smile at her reassuringly, but she looks away. I feel older and more experienced.

I'm brave.

I can't wait for the day when I'll send the first lot of money I've earned back to my brother. They are getting by on the farm, but it's hard for my siblings, especially for Andrei. I yawn and look at my watch, the one I was given by my brother for my 15th birthday. It's 3am at home.

'Where are we?' I ask when the Russian man, who'd

told me about the riches I could earn in Scandinavia, walks past me.

'Shut your face. You want to reach your destination, don't you?'

He barks his words and his eyes are dark and menacing inside the black hood of his sweater.

I nod, a cold shiver running down my spine.

'Then don't ask any questions.'

I can feel the eyes of the other passengers on me, but I don't dare to look at anyone. Why is the man suddenly so angry at me? Has something not gone to plan?

We are all sitting on a small bank. The ground is cold and slightly damp, but I'm glad of the fresh air. After two days and nights on the bus, with just the occasional convenience stop, I was longing for the smell of outdoors instead of the body odors of the people around me.

Everyone is quiet, fearful of the same reaction that I got. Only the two Russians, who are standing farther away, gazing out into the darkness, are talking. They look as if they're waiting for something. Their heads are close together, their voices low. The man I know better, but who's name I haven't been told, has a leather satchel slung across his back. In it, I know, are the passports of all the people on the bus. The Russian said to me, when he collected the money and checked our papers, that it made it easier when crossing borders if he kept all the documents together. It was in my interest and made the journey faster and cheaper.

'You'll get your passport back when we are at our destination,' he said and grinned as if it was a joke.

That's the last time I saw the man smile.

Perhaps he's had some bad news along the way? I noticed that he was on his cell the whole of the journey, talking in the same low voice he's using now with the other man.

Suddenly a new, much smarter coach pulls up in front of the group and the other Russian opens the back door of the vehicle.

'Quick,' he says and motions the group off the grass bank and onto the vehicle.

When I'm introduced to the farm manager, Lars Olen, I am a little afraid. But when the stern-looking tall man shows me into a cottage with a small kitchenette and a bathroom, housing a real shower, and proper beds, I'm relieved. There is even food in the fridge and a bicycle leaning against the wall outside.

The man starts speaking in English. I try to concentrate and manage to understand almost everything the man says.

'You work six days and one day off.' Lars Olen holds up his fingers to illustrate the numbers.

'Understand?'

I nod and try to smile but the expression on the man's face doesn't change.

'On your day off, you can go into town.' The man puts his hand on the bicycle. 'It takes you twenty minutes.'

Again, he lifts his hands up, opening his palms and stretching out his fingers twice.

I try nodding once more, but this time I don't smile.

Now Lars Olen points at a large white building, with a garden around it, across one of the fields.

'That house over there belongs to Mr and Mrs Ulsson. Don't bother them. They own the farm. You talk to me only. Is that understood?'

The man's eyes stare down at me and suddenly I feel scared.

'Yes.'

The man's face relaxes and next he points beyond the large house. I spot something blue in the distance and realize that is the sea. The same sea that we crossed on the ferry. We were told to stay inside the cabins, which I was glad about, because I was so very tired. I had a bunk bed with three other men and we all slept until one of the Russians came to wake us in the night. When we got out, the ferry was rocking and I very nearly lost my balance. Luckily the corridors were narrow and I didn't fall.

It's now morning, with the sun high up in the sky, but I am still so very, very tired. It's difficult to concentrate on the man's words and I try hard not to yawn.

'You can use the sauna when I tell you. There is a rowing boat by the shore which is also for your use. There's still some fish in the sea. There are rods and such. Do you know how to fish?'

I nod even though I have no idea how to fish. But I don't want to disappoint my new boss.

CHAPTER FOUR

Frida has just managed to get Anne Sofie settled for the night when there's a knock on the door. She looks at the time on her phone and hesitates in the hallway. She's not expecting anyone.

It must be Isabelle, an older woman who lives in the house next door. She has been looking after her little kitten, Minki, while Frida was in Sjoland.

She's often asking to borrow something, on a pretext, Frida suspects. She lives on her own, with her children away in Sweden, and she's lonely.

But when Frida opens the door, she's surprised to find a man standing there, in the twilight of the early evening. He looks familiar, and immediately, Frida knows who it is.

'I am Andrei Tamas. You don't know me, but you know my brother,' the man says in heavily accented English.

He's a little taller than Daniel, but he has the same kind eyes and the same facial features with high cheeks and a wide mouth. Although he is a lot more muscular. And handsome.

Frida's stomach flips.

Andrei coughs and looks down at his shoes. He hadn't been prepared for this. On Frida Anttila's Facebook page she had spiky, rainbow colored hair and an angry look in her eyes. He'd been prepared for a defensive, even a bitter person. Instead, here stands a tired-looking, but gorgeous, young woman. She's holding a cloth of some kind in her hand, and the sleeves of her checked shirt are rolled up.

'I'm sorry to interrupt your evening,' Andrei says.

The woman continues to stare at him with those blue eyes of hers.

Suddenly a small black and white cat appears at the woman's feet. It tries to sneak past him, but Andrei crouches down and picks up the creature.

'Where are you going?' Andrei says when he sees that it's just a kitten.

'Thank you!' Frida says. 'She keeps trying to escape, but she's too young to go out yet.'

Andrei smiles down at the kitten, who begins to purr in his arms.

Frida Anttila gazes at both him and the little kitten, now comfortably held against his chest.

'What do you want?' she whispers almost inaudibly.

Again, Andrei hesitates. He hadn't expected this reception, nor is he prepared to reveal everything yet.

'Can I come in?' he asks.

The woman nods and steps aside to let him in. As she closes the door, Andrei gently drops the kitten onto the floor. Immediately it begins to circle his leg.

'She likes you,' Frida says and a smile fleetingly crosses her face. The young woman passes him in the hall, and then asks him to take off his shoes. Andrei looks down at a shelf with hooks for coats and sees below it a rack with several pairs of sneakers in various colors. Next to them are smaller shoes.

A child?

He pulls his trainers off and sees one of his socks has a hole in it. He stretches it over the big toe and down toward the sole, to hide it, but it won't stay there. Shrugging, he follows Frida to a space filled with green plants and light. The kitten flies past him.

The room is vast, with a high ceiling and a large window overlooking similar wooden houses and, beyond them, the sea. The sun is low, but it's still light. At eight o'clock at night.

In the middle of the room is an old-fashioned sofa, with a velour seat and an intricately carved wooden frame. There are two matching chairs opposite the sofa, and a coffee table in between. In the windows and on high pedestals, hang various green plants. The room is stylish, yet it's not all together tidy. In one corner, toys spill from a basket, a baby walker next to it, and different playthings are scattered here and there. A low bookcase on the back wall is filled with children's books, while another, tall one, is brimming with ancient volumes.

Frida is standing next to the window. The light plays

with her short hair and slight frame, making her silhou-ette all but disappear into the scenery outside.

'Would you like some coffee? Tea? Or a drink?'

Andrei hesitates, but then nods. 'A drink would be nice, thank you.'

Frida walks past him and he catches a momentary scent of her. Roses?

CHAPTER FIVE

F rida's hands shake when she reaches into the fridge and pulls out two bottles of Mariestad beer. She flicks the tops off and decides against glasses. The guy looks like someone who would prefer to drink straight from the bottle. Like she does.

She checks that the kitten, who is now sitting at her bowl eating, and still purring loudly, has enough water and food. She thinks how odd it is that the kitten took to this strange man so quickly. She got Minki just a couple of weeks ago, and the kitten hasn't liked anyone who's visited her before.

She'd disappeared underneath the sofa when Alicia came, and hidden from her neighbor.

Frida stands for a moment and gazes out at the view from her small kitchen. The large living room also has a view of the sea. It was this outlook, as well as the safe courtyard for Anne Sofie, that made her buy the apartment on the ground floor of the old wooden house. In summer, Frida loves following the sailing ships, ferries, and various boats as they move in and out of her view. In winter, there are fewer small vessels; just the large cruise ships making their way to and from the West Harbor.

Today, however, she's looking out without seeing anything. She's trying to gather herself.

She knew this day would come. Daniel told her he had a sister and two brothers in Romania. For a long time, while she was still pregnant, she expected a call, a letter, an email, something from his family. But nothing came. And then, unwittingly, she got caught up in Alicia's dreams. For a while, she even believed herself that the baby she was carrying was Stefan's. But it was all a daydream.

She thinks back to those days, when despair and sadness were with her every moment of the day – and night. When she'd see both Stefan and Daniel's faces everywhere.

How she had wished that the baby was Alicia's grandchild! But she couldn't carry on with the pretense forever. Frida shakes her head when she thinks of Alicia's kindness. And Hilda's, her mother. Not very many people would have forgiven her for the deceit, however well-conceived it was. Let alone take her in and make her part of the Ulsson family like they have.

And now Daniel's brother is here.

How will Hilda – herself just recovering from the loss of her beloved husband – and Alicia react to having Anne Sofie's uncle around? And what does the man want? Frida wishes she hadn't opened the door to him, although he is very handsome.

No. Don't even go there!

When Frida steps back into the room, the guy is looking through her books. Or, rather, her mother's old volumes. Hearing her steps, he turns around abruptly, as if she's found him doing something untoward.

'Sit down, please,' Frida says and hands him the bottle.

'Thank you,' Andrei replies, sitting down on the sofa and taking a swig.

Frida notices that he drinks greedily, nearly emptying the bottle.

'Sorry, I am thirsty,' he declares, grinning at Frida.

'No worries.'

She smiles back at him and sits down on one of the chairs opposite the man.

Andrei regards Frida for a moment, as if assessing her.

'Sorry, my English...'

'You're fine,' Frida says quickly.

She wants this over and done with now.

'What do you want with me?' she asks and adds, 'Why are you here?'

The man looks down at his feet and Frida notices that there is a large hole in one of his socks. Quickly, she raises her eyes to his face, but it's too late.

Andrei pulls the visible toe under his other foot.

They look at each other but neither says anything.

Andrei leans forward on the sofa and digs into the back pocket of his jeans. He fiddles with his phone for a moment, then hands it to Frida.

'Do you – or did you – know this boy?'

With a shaking hand, Frida takes hold of the cell and

stares at a laughing Daniel. He's standing outside a bus, with a wide smile on his face. He looks so alive. Tears start running down Frida's cheeks. She doesn't dare look at Andrei, or speak, so she simply nods.

Andrei doesn't say anything. He's learned that with people, just like animals, you do well to give them time. There's no point in rushing the cows back to the milking parlor or hurrying them back out again. They will walk at their own pace. A calf is born when the time is right for the heifer, not before, so there's no need to fret about it.

It's the same with people. His sister Maria would cook when she wanted. If either of them rushed her, hungry from an exhausting day on the farm, she'd take even longer to produce dinner. And Mihai, the more you asked him to be quicker in his tasks, the slower he'd go too.

So Andrei waits until Frida has finished sniffling and wiping her eyes with a tissue, and hands the cell back to him.

'He was a very good friend,' Frida says finally.

Her eyes now have red rims around them and the tip of her nose is slightly pink. Somehow this makes him even more attracted to her.

'Just a friend?' Andrei says, and regrets his words immediately. He puts his hands up and quickly follows up with, 'I'm sorry. That is not my business. I am Daniel's old brother and I am here to find out what happen. What really has happen to my brother Daniel.'

He pulls out the piece of paper he was given by old Grigore Levandovschi what seems like years ago. The days of traveling have taken a toll on him. He hands the document over to Frida and she takes it, but then, without looking at it, asks if he'd like another beer.

Andrei nods and waits until she's back again. In the meantime, the little black and white kitten has come into the room and jumped onto Andrei's lap.

When Frida returns with another bottle of beer, he gazes at her face.

'This came from our police. It's from your authorities,' he states, pointing at the piece of paper. He waits while Frida sits down again and picks it up and reads it.

'It's in Romanian,' Frida says.

Andrei takes back the report and translates it, as best as he can, into English.

'That's what happened,' Frida says, after he's finished reading. She looks as if she's about to burst into tears again, and Andrei doesn't know what to do. He wants to go over and take her in his arms, but he knows this is absurd. The kitten purrs loudly.

'Would you like me to go now?' he says.

Frida widens her eyes for a moment and shakes her head.

'No, it's just...' she takes a deep breath and carries on. 'It was a very difficult time for me. You see, I'd just lost my boyfriend seven months before, and I was still grieving, when... when Daniel had the accident.'

. . .

Frida tells Andrei everything. Well, almost everything. She recounts how she met Stefan, her beautiful Stefan, who died in a motorcycle accident in London. The roads were icy and he lost control. How she and Stefan had started to hang out with Daniel after she'd met him at the library. How she found out she was pregnant after Stefan had gone, and Daniel had promised to look after her, only to then perish at sea. She lost two of her best friends within a year.

She doesn't tell Andrei that Daniel is Anne Sofie's real father. She doesn't know why she lets him believe – just as she did Alicia and Hilda – that the girl is Stefan's.

All through Frida's story, Andrei stares at her intently as he listens. Frida can't look into his eyes. They are so dark and so inviting. She has to control herself. Instead, she gazes at her hands while she speaks, trying to keep her voice level. It keeps failing her and she has to stop on several occasions.

It's been a long time since Frida has spoken at length about that fateful time with anyone. If she even hints at Stefan, both Alicia and Hilda get upset.

In the playground and the nursery that Anne Sofie attends two days a week, she tells the other parents that Anne Sofie's dad isn't around. She doesn't elaborate and people don't ask. Some, she knows, are aware of her story – it's not every day a body is found in the archipelago. Alicia, then working as a reporter on the local paper, had been true to her word and kept her name out of the papers, but people still talk.

It's a small island community.

There is a silence when Frida finishes speaking. The

room has darkened, and she gets up and switches on the two lamps set either side of the wide window. She comes back to her seat and faces Andrei.

'But my brother. What really happen with Daniel?' he asks.

There is a stillness in the room.

'Exactly what it says there,' Frida replies, and chin nods toward the crumpled piece of paper on the coffee table between them.

She scans Andrei's face.

Why are you really here?

CHAPTER SIX

'You don't mind?' Alicia asks.

She's standing in her mother's kitchen, watching Hilda's back, as the older woman lifts a pan out of soapy water.

They've just had dinner, a routine they've fallen into since Alicia moved into the converted milking parlor.

Her mom turns around and smiles, 'I said I don't. He is your father after all.'

Alicia considers her mom for a moment longer. She can detect a tightness in her voice.

'I tell you what, Mom, let's just book him into the Arkipelag. It'll be awkward for him too, being under the same roof as you. I'd have him in the cottage, but you know there's only one room, and I'm not sure I'm prepared to share. I've only met Leo a handful of times, so ...'

Hilda comes over to where Alicia is sitting on her favorite stool by the corner of the kitchen and wipes her wet hands on her apron. 'Stop! I said he can stay here.

I've got more than enough room. And he is only staying for two nights, right?'

Alicia nods.

'I was married to him once upon a time, so he's not a complete stranger. Besides, you're across the yard, so it really isn't an issue.'

Once back in her cottage, sitting in the nook of her corner sofa, Alicia gazes out to sea. She has an uninterrupted view of the water. There's a couple of small outcrops nearby and a larger island in the distance. Today, there's a strong wind and the surface of the water ripples with waves, and there's a thin orange strip visible on the horizon where the sun has already set. It's getting dark.

Alicia thinks about how here, in the islands, she notices even the smallest change in weather, as well as light. The dimness when winter is upon them, to the nightless nights of June. And in between, this slow but definite move from the long summer days to the short days of fall, and back again. At the moment, in August, the nights are drawing in, but Alicia doesn't mind. She's almost looking forward to the chill of winter.

When she lived in London, her only concern was whether it was raining or not. The different seasons seemed to blend into each other.

With her laptop open, Alicia is trying to compose a reply to her father, answering his query about the visit to Åland. They've been emailing a lot, especially since Leo had a heart bypass operation in May. His recovery has been remarkable, helped no doubt by his newfound sobriety. He's lost a lot of weight too and has even started going to the gym.

She's been to see Leo twice in Helsinki, staying in a hotel. During those visits, they've grown closer. Alicia has learned more about his life, and about the short courtship and marriage with her mother, which led to her birth. They've even spoken more about how and why the relationship between Leo and Hilda broke down.

Alicia has told her father about her own life, including the recent tumultuous events. She's painted a picture of her wonderful son, who was only seventeen when he lost his life in the motorbike accident. Having met Leo for the first time last summer, she now knows that Stefan carried a strong resemblance to his grandfather. The mop of blond hair, the strong jaw, the blue eyes, and his solid physique were all from Leo. Even though talking about Stefan still tears her heart out, it's also been wonderful to relive his life through talking about him with her dad.

She's been able to open up about her own marriage to Liam too. She's explained to her father how difficult it was to keep going after Stefan's death, and how, in the end, their union couldn't take the strain of their bereavement. For some reason, she's not been able to tell Leo about Liam's unfaithfulness. But she has told him about Patrick.

Patrick.

Alicia sighs when she thinks about Patrick. Although he hasn't said so, she thinks Leo doesn't like Patrick.

They've met only once, at a time when Alicia's life was again in turmoil.

Alicia doesn't know whether it's Leo's old-fashioned views, but he seemed a lot more positive about Liam. When Alicia mentioned during one of their FaceTime calls that she is still in contact with Liam, her dad had nodded approvingly and said, 'That's good.'

Alicia had been annoyed with him.

'As friends,' she'd added.

'Yes, course!'

Leo had sounded convincing, but his facial expression spoke another truth.

'It's a shame you never met.'

Alicia wanted to point out how absurd it was that Leo was taking Liam's side. Not that there were any sides, because she and Liam had separated and were about to start divorce proceedings. Alicia needs to remind Liam to get the papers ready. But she hasn't yet. She's just been too busy with the farm.

CHAPTER SEVEN

Alicia's thoughts are interrupted by a knock on the door.

A man's voice calls out, 'Miss Ulsson, can I have a word?'

It's the farm manager, Lars Olen.

'I wanted to talk to you about labor,' he says.

'Come into the kitchen,' Alicia says, pointing at one of the four chairs around a pale oak table. 'Lars, please sit down. Would you like a coffee, or something stronger? I have beer, wine or whiskey.'

'Oh, thank you, Miss,'

'Alicia please, how many times do I have to tell you?' Alicia grins at the man who's still standing by the door.

'Which is it to be?'

Lars moves slowly inside and perches on a chair.

'A beer,' he says.

'So, are we short of men for the potato harvest? I thought we managed alright with old Jonsson for the spring crops?'

'Ah, you see that's the problem. He's old. And very slow. I've taken a look at the books and the harvest costs were nearly 25 percent less with two hands instead of one.'

Alicia gazes at Lars's face, which has deep lines around his mouth and forehead. His arms are bronzed by the summer's sunshine, and his fair hair is almost gray now. His deep-set eyes are downcast, looking at the bottle of beer he's holding between his knees. Alicia knows, without even seeing his expression what this discussion is all about. And she can also guess what he thinks – or hopes – the outcome is.

'What's your solution?' Alicia asks even though she knows the answer.

Now the farm manager lifts his head and gazes directly at Alicia.

'Your dad, or step-dad, I beg your pardon, used Eastern European boys every year. We had them from the spring up to the fall. They're good workers, they're fast, and with the cottage for them to live in, they're very happy. The conditions here are far better than anywhere else and that's why they like it here. We take good care of them.'

Alicia sighs.

'And we pay them less than Jonsson.'

Lars takes a swig out of his beer and wipes his mouth on the back of his hand.

'We pay the going rate, even a bit more, I believe,' he says.

'But the cottage isn't available anymore. It's part of Mom's rentals,' Alicia points out, although she thinks

Hilda's new business has got off to a slow start. All the same, it's not fair on her mother for Alicia to requisition one of the largest assets of her new business.

'Hmm,' Lars says and drinks more of his beer.

'What about local lads?' Alicia asks.

Lars snorts.

'They're all off to Stockholm or even farther away as soon as they leave school. Unless they're already studying in Sweden, in which case they stay on. Besides, you know the last place the youngsters want to work is a farm, pulling up potatoes! If they come back for the summer, it's either a cafe or the ferries they want to be on.'

Lars finishes his drink and gets up.

'Well, have a think about it. But we don't have much time. Usually, we're in full swing by now and we need help out there. The plants are already in bud and will be in flower soon, ready for lifting,' he says, and turns to leave Alicia alone, wondering how she will pacify both Lars and keep hold of her own principles.

After the farm manager has left, Alicia pours herself a large glass of white wine. She remains seated at the kitchen table thinking about her stepdad, Uffe. How she wishes she could ask for his help right now!

She knows most farmers in Åland use temporary foreign labor, perfectly legally, and she also knows that Uffe used to pay the young men in cash rather than put the salaries through the accounts. How he got away with it year after year, Alicia has no idea. She's determined to keep everything above board with the farm.

What's more, she's not quite sure where Uffe got his labor from. She should have asked Lars, she now realizes. If he came to see her, he must already have a solution, even new farm hands lined up already. Briefly, she considers giving him a call, but then thinks that it would be better to do that face to face. Tomorrow morning will do.

Poor Daniel's dead body flashes in front of her eyes. He was one of the previous summer's workers from Romania. When convalescing from a nasty accident on the farm, he'd gone fishing and capsized his boat and drowned. It was sad enough that he'd been working on Uffe's farm, but he'd been good friends with Frida, Stefan's girlfriend.

Later, it turned out that it was Daniel who had fathered Frida's daughter, and not Stefan, as the girl had initially claimed. Still, Alicia considered herself little Anne Sofie's grandma, just as she had when the little girl was born.

She understood how, faced with her own and Alicia's grief over Stefan's sudden death, followed by Daniel's demise, Frida had wanted to believe that Stefan had fathered the child.

Alicia knew bereavement could make people do strange things. She herself had started a passionate affair with a Swedish reporter last summer.

Alicia takes another large mouthful of wine. She hasn't seen Patrick for over two weeks now and hasn't spoken to him for days. Last weekend he had to work and Alicia couldn't leave the farm to take the ferry to Stockholm. Somehow, Alicia can feel a wedge building between them. They've even stopped phoning each other every night.

She picks up her cell and begins to dial his number, but presses end half-way through. She needs to clear her head for the farm affairs tomorrow. Patrick can wait. Instead, she dials a London number.

CHAPTER EIGHT

'Hello you,' Liam says softly after he's seen the name on the screen of his cell.

'Can you talk or are you just about to go into theatre?'

Liam loves the fact that Alicia is always so conscious of his career as a surgeon.

'No, you're OK. I don't have any more ops today. But can you hang on just a minute, though?'

Liam is in the middle of seeing his out-patients, but he decides to take a break, so he can talk to Alicia. He gets up from behind his desk and goes to open the door. In the hallway, he spots the back of his new assistant.

'Clare, can I take five before Mrs ...'

Liam racks his brain for the name of his next patient, but his assistant, a young woman with an open face and very short hair, comes to his rescue.

'Mrs White is running late, so you have no one for the next ten minutes or so.'

'Excellent, thank you!'

Liam retreats to his room and locks the door behind him. The nurses always knock, but he doesn't want to take the risk of one of them opening the door by mistake and interrupting his conversation with Alicia.

'Sorry about that. How are you? How are things on the farm?'

'I don't know, Liam. Sometimes I wonder if I made a huge mistake.'

'Nonsense. You are very capable, but why do you say that?'

Alicia tells Liam about Lars's suggestion.

'Is this about Daniel? His accident had nothing to do with working for Uffe, did it?'

Liam knows that the Romanian boy's death so close to the time when they lost Stefan affected Alicia deeply.

'Yes and no. I guess I just want everything to be above board. And I don't know if Uffe paid the boys under the table, so to speak. And Mom won't tell me anything.'

Alicia's voice falters, and Liam wishes he was on the islands now, sitting with her. He could take her into his arms – if she would let him – and tell her that everything will be alright. They could discuss the problem through properly together. Liam is convinced there is a good solution to most things in life.

After she's put the phone down, Alicia feels better. More energized and positive. Liam pointed out that there's always more than one way to do things, and Alicia knows he's right. Liam had suggested cutting costs somewhere else or even diversifying to allow her to employ the more expensive local labor.

She doesn't know how she can do that. The large potato chip company on the islands, Krisp, runs a very tight operation. They pay every farmer the same price for the harvest, depending on the market price at the time. The spring harvest revenue is always a little better, because not all the farmers on the islands produce two crops of potatoes. Uffe has concentrated on potatoes for years now. Alicia remembers him telling her that the small size of his fields made potatoes the best crop to grow. It wasn't worth diversifying.

Still, there must be something she can do to increase the amount of money they can get for the potatoes.

Alicia takes a sip of wine and turns back to her computer. She's going to do some research before she takes Lars's advice. It can't be the only way.

CHAPTER NINE

L iam is exhausted after another ten-hour day. He's grateful for his short commute from St Mary's hospital to his new apartment in one of the 1930s red-brick blocks in St John's Wood. Although he misses the house he shared with Alicia, in the end it was a relief to leave the semi-detached property in Crouch End. The house had so many memories. Sitting in the empty rooms on his own in the evenings and waking in the double bed at the start of the day made Liam go nearly crazy with longing. He missed his teenage son in a way that was almost impossible to artic-ulate, but the yearning he had for his wife was also unbearable. He could hardly manage both.

Alicia.

He checks his phone, but his last WhatsApp message from Alicia was earlier that day, after their phone conversation. It's too late to talk to her now, as it'll be past midnight in Sjoland. He'll phone her first thing tomorrow morning.

Liam is grateful for the friendship that has formed between them in the past few months. It's as if being thousands of miles apart has brought them closer together.

This gives Liam hope.

He knows he is the reason their marriage ended. Or their separation began. They are still officially married, although they'd agreed to start divorce proceedings. But Liam can't bring himself to do it, and Alicia hasn't so far asked about it. Selling the house was always going to be the first step. Now that their assets have been divided, Liam's lawyer says it's just a matter of signing the papers to make the separation official.

But he has other plans.

Liam is buoyed by Alicia's decision to stay on the islands rather than go back to Stockholm and the Swedish journalist. While he thinks Patrick and Alicia are still seeing each other, Alicia hardly mentions him. It can't help that Patrick is in Stockholm pursuing his own career.

Alicia's decision not to go to Stockholm reopens the door to him, because she obviously doesn't love Patrick as much as she loves the islands. If she had given up the farm for Patrick, he would have tried to forget about Alicia. And Alicia has let slip that Patrick slept with his ex while Alicia was back on the islands, supporting her mother after Uffe's death.

Liam knows that it's stupid to think this way, but he can't help believe that the Swede's actions have put the two of them on equal footing. They have both been unfaithful to Alicia. But Liam is going to show Alicia, through his actions, how much he still loves her. If she can forgive him, there is hope of a future together.

As he opens the door to his one-bedroom apartment, Liam smiles to himself. His last lesson with the Swedish teacher had gone better than he'd anticipated. He is able to converse with Katarina after only three months of sessions. He cannot understand why he never tried to learn the language before. He was too busy building his career, but such a small commitment to Alicia's heritage – and Stefan's too – would have made a huge difference to them as a family. He is certain of this now.

Grinning to himself, Liam thinks how not being able to converse with his mother-in-law had been a bonus. But again, that was a silly way of thinking.

He plans to become good enough to impress Alicia when he goes to see her in Sjoland.

That's step one.

Step two is to remind her of how much they loved each other. He has been thinking a lot about that cold weekend in Uppsala at the Swedish university where they met. Alicia was a young student and he was playing hooky at a boring medical conference when Alicia came to sit at the same table as him in the student canteen. It was love at first sight, and the next day they'd kissed and made love in Alicia's tiny student digs. He was lost to Alicia there and then.

But then, eighteen years later they lost Stefan in a motorcycle accident. They couldn't cope with the grief. And Liam couldn't cope with the guilt.

It was he who had encouraged his son to buy a motorcycle. It was he who had let Stefan borrow Alicia's stepfather's moped on the islands when he was just sixteen. That moped, which could barely do 40 miles an hour, was the start of his son's obsession with motorcycles of all kinds. For Liam, it meant that Stefan was growing up. For Alicia, it meant night terrors when she feared he'd have an accident. A fear that came horribly true.

To cope with all that guilt, Liam broke his marriage vows and sought refuge elsewhere.

What a stupid, stupid man!

Liam opens the doors to his balcony overlooking the lush communal gardens between his block and the house opposite. Both houses belong to the same development, which forms a square. It was the Art Deco style of the apartments that appealed to Liam, as well as the location, so close to his hospital.

The square is almost like a private park. At this time of year, in August, it's a riot of blooms. Some white flowers, which Liam cannot identify (horticulture isn't his forte) shine attractively in the otherwise dark garden. It was a surprise to Liam how much comfort he gets at the beginning and end of each day from sitting on the small balcony, watching the gardens and listening to birdsong, though this is absent now. He can hear the faint traffic noise from the busy Finchley Road behind the block opposite. Liam thanks his luck to have an apartment in the quieter block, away from the busy London thoroughfare.

Liam's thoughts return to Alicia and his plan to show her that he has changed. He wants to prove to her that their marriage hasn't totally broken down. Or that it can't be mended.

When Liam last saw her, about three months ago, during her stepfather's funeral, he'd planned to ask her to consider returning to London. But when he saw her, he realized she loved the islands and would never leave them again.

At the time, Liam thought he felt the same way about his work at the hospital and London. But his months alone have convinced him that he can change his life. After all, Alicia gave up her home to marry him. She has given up so much during their marriage: her home, her career, her heritage, her family, and her son.

It's time for Liam to redress the balance.

CHAPTER TEN

Leo is making his way up to the ship's viewing platform, together with youngsters carrying backpacks and families with excited children, two of whom overtake him on the narrow ladder leading out of the car decks.

One of the boys drops something and Leo sees it's a battered-looking teddy bear.

'You might need that later,' he says, turning to a pretty young woman, who seems to be the boys' mom. She smiles at him.

'Thank you so much! You've saved a drama at bedtime.'

Leo grins back at the young woman.

'And sorry about the rush. They've been in the car for far too long,' she adds apologetically as she walks briskly past him to catch up with her brood of two boys and a little girl.

'No need to apologize!'

Leo means what he says. He knows what young kids

are like. He doesn't mind them. He rather enjoys their enthusiasm, because it matches his own. He's just not able to show it quite so energetically as the youngsters.

As he reaches the deck, the fresh air hits him and the wind whips up his thinning hair. He takes a cap out of his back pocket and pulls it firmly down on his head. He's at the back of the ferry, and when he finds an unoccupied part of the railing, he looks up at the receding outline of Helsinki.

A smile hovers on his lips when he looks at his city, basking in the summer heat. The domes of the cathedral shine green as the sun's rays hit its copper roof, tarnished over time. It stands proud over the neoclassical buildings in front of it. There's the President's Palace and then the busy, messy market in front, red canvas covering the stalls. A lump forms in his throat when he thinks about the beauty of the world, which he so nearly left too early. He's been given a second bite of the apple, and he's determined to enjoy it to its fullest.

Leo's thoughts turn immediately to Alicia, his strong, brave, beautiful daughter. Without her, he would have perished last year, carried on drinking, smoking, and not taking care of himself. It was she who gave him the courage to change his life-long habits, which in turn enabled him to get the operation he needed.

Now, three months later, he can walk without running out of breath, even take a few stairs – slowly – and live a life that he should have had from the beginning. Immediately, he changes the train of his thoughts.

No regrets.

That's his mantra now. He listened to the psychiatrists assigned to him after the heart bypass. He nearly declined the sessions, but then thought about Alicia and decided to give it a go.

'Concentrate on what you can change and don't dwell on things that are not under your control,' the man had told him.

Once in the bar, Leo can't ignore the past. He remembers how last spring, three months ago now, he sat at the counter, drinking pint after pint of beer. There'd been Jaegermeister chasers too, even though he'd promised himself to stay sober for what he feared would be the last time he'd see his daughter.

And Hilda.

Of course, he couldn't keep off the booze then. He now understands that he probably is an alcoholic, and as hard as it has been, he hasn't touched a drop in four months, four days and – he checks his watch – ten hours.

'What can I get you?' the burly barman asks.

'Do you have any non-alcoholic beers?'

The man runs down a list and Leo chooses his favorite, Koff Nikolai, while he eyes the range of beers on tap. Before his thoughts turn to *surely one wouldn't hurt* territory, he takes the bottle and the glass the barman has given him, leaves the cash on the counter, and goes back outside.

He knew this trip, the first since that fateful one last year to see Alicia in Åland, would make him nervous. More so after the email received from Alicia last night, telling him that Leo was 'more than welcome' to stay in Sjoland. With Hilda.

My new cottage is across the yard, as you know, but there's only one room, so I thought you'd be more comfortable in the large house. Hilda rents rooms to guests in the summer, but there is a free suite just now which I'd love you to stay in.

Leo wanted to offer to pay but thought this might insult Alicia and Hilda. That's the last thing he wants to do. He's looking forward to seeing Hilda again, but living under her roof is going to be awkward, to say the least. It's not that he doesn't want to show her how much he has changed, but the guilt he carries about the past is too overwhelming.

Being sober has its disadvantages, he thinks and gives a sarcastic grin into the bottle of alcohol-free beer.

CHAPTER ELEVEN

W ho would have known that the summer on these islands is so very nice? The work is hard, and the hours long, but I don't mind. It's almost like being at home, except someone else than Andrei tells me what to do. And there's no Mihai or Maria. But I sleep well in the little cottage, where I have my own room.

Another man, Florian, who is a few years older than me, also from Romania, although from north of the country, turned up a week after I had settled into the farm routine. He tells me that I am lucky, that Mr Ulsson's farm is one of the better ones.

At first, I don't understand what Florian means, but the guy is the quiet type, and I don't want to appear green by asking too many questions.

We both work hard all week, sometimes putting in ten or twelve hours, but sometimes we have the whole weekend off.

On the Friday evening of the first week with Florian,

when we are having a beer in the cottage and watching the TV with programs in the incomprehensible Swedish language, I glance at the older man. He has a mop of black hair on his head and strong features with dark, almost black eyes. His forehead is high, making him look intelligent.

'How many years have you worked for Mr Ulsson?' I ask after our second beer.

Florian gives me a stare.

'What's it to you?' He grunts and moves his eyes back toward the TV.

The older man is lying on a sofa set against the long wall of the cottage, while I sit on a green recliner.

'I just wondered how long it takes to pay back the cost of the journey. One of the Russians told me that ...'

Florian interrupts me.

'Don't talk about those bastards to me. Or anyone else for that matter.'

'I don't understand ...'

Florian turns his face away from the TV again and sits up. His dark eyes are on me. Pointing his beer bottle toward me, he asks, 'How old are you?'

'Sixteen.'

My voice rises at the beginning of the word and I'm embarrassed. Now the older man will think I'm just a kid.

Florian shakes his head and, looking down at his bottle of beer, mutters something. Then, he looks up at me again.

'This place is the best, but they only take you for the summer season. Which is short. In September, you'll be

sent to Stockholm, or Malmö in Southern Sweden, where you'll be cleaning offices, smart homes or factories. If you keep your head down, they might send you back here. But if you create trouble, or ask too many questions ...'

Florian makes a gesture with his hand, as if cutting his own throat.

'But I thought all I needed to do was work until I pay back the cost of the trip and the paperwork to get here. They told me ...'

Again, the older man interrupts me.

'For fuck's sake, I know you're young and green, but you must know that's bullshit, right?'

I say nothing. But my mind is whirling with questions. I've heard the horror stories. Glancing sideways at Florian I wonder if I dare to talk about them with Florian. I decide it's best not to.

Perhaps Florian has read my mind, because he lifts himself up and pats me on the shoulder.

'It's not so bad here, is it? And look at me, I'm healthy and happy, right?'

Florian turns toward the small kitchenette and asks over his shoulder, 'Another beer?'

It's now winter and I'm in the small apartment in Stockholm, sleeping in one room with four other young men like me. I fall asleep thinking back to the summer months in Åland, where I felt almost free.

I work hard and hope that I will be allowed to return to the summer island soon.

I do as the Russians tell me, cleaning offices or houses at dawn. We only get to sleep a few hours during the day, and then we return to the backbreaking factory work before I get picked up to start the early cleaning jobs again.

This is not the life I planned, but today, in the middle of the winter in Stockholm when the city is covered in snow, the Russian tells me that I've nearly paid off my transfer costs.

I am so tired but the thought that soon I will get my passport back and then I'll be free keeps me going.

When they tell me I'm going back to the Ulsson's farm, I try hard to hide how happy the news makes me.

The Russian looks into my face and says, 'You want to go?'

I nod, trying not to seem too enthusiastic. I've learned to do what Florian told me last summer. Keep my head down and say as little as possible.

'They liked you there. But remember,' here the man comes close to me and I can smell his sour breath. 'Do as they say and work hard.'

'Yes.' I reply, loudly now, so that he knows I will be good.

I want to ask him how long I have left to pay off my debt, but a new man, who has been cleaning a large office with me asked that a few weeks ago and he got a slap across his face. So, I remain quiet and keep my fingers crossed behind my back. Perhaps going back to the Ulsson's farm is a good sign?

CHAPTER TWELVE

Andrei wakes up to the light streaming into his room. He registers voices. A little girl giggling and the young woman, Frida, talking to her in soft tones.

Andrei looks around himself. This is a comfortable room, with a vast bed and an oriental rug on a dark, wooden floor. All around him are signs of wealth. The bed, the little side table, the bookcase, all of it seems new, apart from an old chest of drawers standing underneath the window. The see-through drapes flap lazily in the draft, and Andrei sees that the window is slightly open at the side. From his vantage point on the bed, he can see blue sky above, with the sun high up, bathing the room in sunlight. He gets up and yawns, thinking first, how can a young single mother afford such a place right bang in the middle of the town, and second, he could get used to living in a place like this. He thinks back to the farmhouse, with its boarded floors, wooden beds with ancient mattresses filled with horse hair. And then he thinks of the open space, his cows, his brother and sister. His duty to look after them.

He puts on his pants and T-shirt and opens the door to the hallway, where Frida showed him where the bathroom was. Before going in, he carries on along the hallway, following a smell of something lovely and the continuing exchanges between the baby and the woman. He stops at the doorway to the kitchen where Frida is feeding a little girl in a highchair, waving her arms and feet about. The whole of her face is covered in some kind of white stuff – porridge Andrei assumes.

'Good morning,' Frida says, looking up at him with an open smile on her face.

Andrei takes in the scene. Mother and baby are both happy, as if they were sharing a joke. The kitchen table is filled with toys, a large cup of coffee and a couple of dishes of baby food. It's messy, with plates and cups piled high in the sink, but Andrei is amazed at how large the space is. He saw a glimpse of it yesterday, but it was dark and he didn't take in how modern it was.

He's stunned by all the electrical goods. There's a dishwasher, something his sister has been dreaming about for as long as he can remember. The door to the machine is open, with the top shelf empty and the bottom bit full of clean dishes. He also spots a food mixer on the top (another item on Maria's wish list) and a coffee maker in the corner, which explains the delicious smell.

Frida follows Andrei's gaze.

'Coffee?'

'Yes, thank you. But first ...' Andrei nods toward the

bathroom door behind him. He picks up the kitten, which has begun to rub itself against his leg. He scratches her behind the ears for a moment and then puts her down.

'Ah, of course. There are towels on the bench in there. Just help yourself.'

Frida's cheeks color slightly, which makes Andrei smile.

'Thank you,' he says and moves backwards.

'She likes you!' Frida shouts after Andrei, as the kitten follows him closely.

As he imagined, the towels left for him by Frida are soft and fluffy. He does his ablutions, and returns, washed and shaved to the kitchen.

The baby is now on the floor, crawling about, dodging chair and table legs, as she makes her way toward a pile of bright plastic cups, arranged in a tower. Frida is busy in the kitchen, putting things away while her eyes follow her daughter. Hearing his footsteps, she turns around and smiles.

'Did you sleep well?'

'Yes, thank you. You have very nice home.'

Frida gazes at him with an expression he can't decipher but says nothing. Instead, she pours him a cup of coffee and points at a selection of meats, cheeses, and cucumber cut into neat slices, and a basket filled with various kinds of bread.

'You must be starving. You've slept for over ten hours.'

Frida doesn't wait for Andrei's reply, but picks up a bottle of milk and lifts up the little girl. 'She's due for her nap. I won't be long.'

When she's left the room, Andrei picks up two pieces of dark rye bread and fills his plate with everything on offer. He's suddenly ravenous. He didn't really eat much on the journey, just the two meat pies and the thermos flask of tea that Maria had packed for him. Fortunately, the coaches had free water in a large container, so he had helped himself to it.

When he's eaten all the bread in the basket and finished almost all the meats, Frida comes back into the room and sits opposite him across the table. At the same time, the kitten hops onto Andrei's lap.

'You can put her down if she's bothering you.'

Frida glances at the cat.

Andrei shakes his head.

'No, it's fine.'

The little creature makes a nest for herself on Andrei's lap and begins to purr.

'So, you wanted to know more about Daniel?'

'You tell me what happen. My brother fight and lose?' Andrei asks the young woman in front of him. He is trying to ignore her attractiveness, the blonde hair and the bright blue eyes, which speak of hidden sorrow, just like his own. He'd like to take the girl to bed, but he knows this is not what he should be thinking about now. He is here to find out what happened to his brother.

'No,' Frida says. 'There was an accident on the farm. The tractor reversed over his foot.'

Andrei considers the woman's words. Daniel grew up

on a farm. Their father had a tractor, an old Russian one, which was always breaking down. Both Andrei and Daniel became experts at repairing the decrepit vehicle, whether it was the breaks failing, a fan belt needing to be replaced, or the crankshaft failing. Andrei can't imagine his little brother being stupid enough to stand too close to a tractor when someone else is driving it.

He sees the young woman hesitate. She's biting her lip and tucking her blonde hair behind her ears.

'Who is driving? Who do this to my brother?'

Andrei can hear his voice has risen, and he sees Frida's eyes widen. His tone disturbs the kitten and it jumps down from his lap.

Don't scare the girl, for the love of God!

He doesn't know what to say to try to calm her, so again, he waits.

'Uffe was there, but I think it was the other farm laborer who was driving. I don't know his name.'

Frida's eyes are sincere, so Andrei believes her.

'OK,' he says. 'And accident on the lake?'

'Sea,' Frida says.

Andrei nods. He thinks about Daniel's letters where he talked about his life on the islands. He'd written that he liked fishing, and how proud he was that he had learned how to row.

You would like it here, brother.

Why hadn't Andrei made the trip sooner? When Daniel was still alive? When he could still have been able to prevent his death.

Andrei rubs his chin.

He'd been worried about his own farm, of course.

Mihai was so very young and Maria so ... what's the word? Impressionable. That's it. There were plenty of boys and grown men in the village who would have taken advantage of Andrei's absence. Maria was beautiful like their mother, but she was too young to settle down.

Worry for his siblings, alone on the farm, suddenly overwhelms Andrei, and he reaches for his cup of coffee to remove the lump that has risen to his throat. He's been in touch with both of them via WhatsApp, but it's not the same as being there with them.

He'll telephone the police station and talk to old Grigore Levandovschi. Perhaps he could drive his motorcycle to the farm and check up on Maria and Mihai.

CHAPTER THIRTEEN

Frida considers the dark-haired man sitting across her kitchen table. She can see the pain of loss etched onto his features. Last night, when he turned up on her doorstep, she'd been glad that at last she could tell Daniel's family everything about him. To someone who would share her grief.

But overnight, and during the morning, while Daniel's brother slept, she became afraid of what would happen if she really told all.

'Ok, accident with tractor and one at sea? Two accidents?'

Frida hears Andrei's harsh tone. She understands but is unable to comment on Daniel's brother's evident sarcasm, which shines through in spite of his slightly faltering English.

'This is not possible. Daniel grow up on farm, and he fishing here all the time. He tell me this in letters ...'

'He told you what?' Frida says before she has time to think.

Andrei leans toward her across the breakfast things still sitting in between them and rests his dark eyes on her.

Suddenly she feels her heart beating harder. Why is it that the first guy she finds even a little attractive happens to be Daniel's brother? Her baby's uncle? Someone who could make her happy, secure life to come tumbling down like a house of cards. What would he say if she told him who Anne Sofie's father and grandfather are?

'What really happen to my brother?'

'I don't know. The police found him on an island in the archipelago,' here Frida involuntarily stretches her hand out toward the glimmering sea outside her window. 'And when they investigated, they found he'd had an accident. The cast of his leg was heavy, and he lost his balance.'

'Oh yeah?'

Again, Frida can hear the doubt in Andrei's voice.

'Honestly, that's all I know. I didn't even see him after. There was no family, so Alicia, I think, recognized him and made the official identification. Together with Uffe.'

Frida feels close to tears now. Reliving that awful time, when pregnant, with Daniel promising to look after both her and the baby, while she was lying about the father to all and sundry. She knew it was wrong, but she didn't want Daniel to be the baby's father. She loved Stefan, and even now, she sometimes thinks of Anne Sofie as Stefan's baby.

'Look, I don't know any more. You need to talk to the police.'

Andrei gets up and fetches something. He returns holding the same piece of paper he'd shown her last night.

'Ebba Torstensson?'

Stretching out the hand holding the report, he jabs at the police chief's name with the forefinger of his other hand.

'How much money I need to give the police here?'

'What? You don't need to give Ebba anything. Just go to the police station and ask to speak with her. She's very nice.'

Frida is shocked to hear that Andrei thinks the police are corrupt. On Åland! She finds the address of Mariehamn police HQ on her cell and shows it to Andrei.

'OK,' Andrei bends down to look at Frida's phone and writes the details into his own cell, tapping quickly with his two thumbs.

'Thank you.'

Andrei's tone is softer now. He's still kneeling next to Frida and their faces are very close to each other. Frida can smell aftershave and something else, a masculine woody scent.

Suddenly the image of gentle Daniel flashes in front of Frida. She struggles to control herself and a tear runs down her cheek. She wipes it with the back of her hand.

The sight of her distress seems to shock Andrei and he brings his hand very close to Frida's so that the sides of their little fingers touch. For a moment, both stare at the table and their two hands resting there, side by side.

Andrei lifts his eyes toward Frida and she notices

that his features have dissolved into a gentleness that she saw when he first picked up the little kitten.

He says, in a quieter voice, 'I'm sorry, I need to know what happen to my little brother.'

'I miss him too,' Frida whispers, gazing at Andrei's face.

They stare at each other for what seems like forever.

Frida is aware of the curve of his mouth, and a thought of how his full lips would taste crosses her mind. Andrei moves closer to Frida but at that moment, the kitten is back, jumping onto Andrei's lap, making him nearly lose his balance.

'Kitty!' Andrei says and gets up to return to his seat opposite Frida.

'Her name is Minki and she has a serious crush on you,' Frida exclaims, trying gently to move the animal away.

'What is this crush?'

Andrei gets up, holding the kitten against his chest with just one hand. Something flips in Frida's mind again and she imagines what it would feel like to rest herself against Andrei's wide chest.

Frida shakes her head and smiles. 'I think she is in love with you.'

Andrei's face turns from slight puzzlement to embarrassment in a matter of seconds. Frida can even see a slight coloring of his cheeks as if he was blushing.

With her grin widening, Frida turns her head away from Andrei so that he can't see her amusement. She goes over to a low kitchen cupboard and takes out the cat food. This arouses the kitten's interest, and she jumps playfully toward her bowl.

'I didn't think kittens could be so characterful,' she says to change the subject, glancing across the kitchen toward Andrei.

He seemed to have overcome his discomposure. 'All animals are.'

He takes a few steps toward Frida, so that he is standing very close to her.

Frida can see the faint stubble on his chin and the dark ring around his brown irises. His eyebrows are as dark as his hair and his lips are lifted slightly in one corner.

'And people too. They are all same. People and animals.'

Andrei's eyes are looking at her so intensely that Frida's breath catches in her throat. She finds herself gazing at his lips as Andrei lowers them to meet hers.

Suddenly there's a cry coming from Anne Sofie's bedroom.

For the first time since the very early baby days, when Anne Sofie had to be fed several times a night, Frida registers disappointment that her daughter is waking up.

Andrei too, hears the sounds, and straightens up.

'As much as I'd like to carry on our conversation about Minki, I'd better get her,' Frida says, smiling.

Andrei nods.

Frida has the overwhelming desire to just give him a light peck on his cheek. Instead, she quickly puts her arms around his torso and gives him a quick hug.

At her touch, Andrei's body tenses. Frida pulls herself away, as if he'd burned her.

Walking across the hall to her daughter's bedroom, Frida wants to pinch herself. What made her touch him like that?

CHAPTER FOURTEEN

When Frida enters Anne Sofie's little room, she sees the girl is already wide awake and playing with the soft toys in the cot. A sweet smile spreads over her face when she sees her mother, and Frida is immediately filled with both utter happiness and terrible guilt. How could she not want to see her daughter? This precious new person should be the center of her world, not some foreign man for whom she feels a passing infatuation!

'Mamma, mamma!' Anne Sofie calls out, stretching her round little arms toward her.

'Mammas lilla sötnos,' Frida coos, picking the baby up and holding onto her tightly.

But as soon as she's out of the cot, Anne Sofie starts to wriggle in her mother's arms. She's just learned to crawl and gets around the apartment with surprising speed.

'Hold on, little one,' Frida says and lays the girl on her back on the floor where she's set out the diaper changing station. Luckily her daughter has inherited Daniel's quiet disposition, and Frida is able to distract the baby from her immediate desire to get moving by offering her favorite toy – a stripy rag doll that Alicia gave her when she was born.

Frida undresses and changes the girl's diaper efficiently with practiced hands. She's glad of the brief moment of respite, away from Andrei, when she can gather her thoughts and settle her breathing. What was she thinking of? Getting the hots for Daniel's brother is a very bad idea. A very bad idea indeed.

Frida grabs a pair of leggings and a matching cotton dress from a drawer above the baby's head and dresses the little girl. Anne Sofie lets her brush the thin wisps of her blonde hair without complaint, and when Frida lifts her up again, she lets her carry her to the kitchen. She's still occupied with the rag doll, pulling at its blonde hair, made out of yellow woollen threads.

When she re-enters the kitchen, Frida doesn't look at Andrei. Instead, she settles the girl in her high chair and goes to prepare a snack for the baby. She's got her back to both Andrei and the baby when she hears him speak to Anne Sofie.

'Hello!'

Frida brings a few pieces of rye bread and a pot of yogurt to the table. Usually, the sight of food makes the baby kick her legs in excitement, but this time she's so focused on Andrei, she doesn't notice what her mom is holding. The girl is staring at Andrei, as if is some kind of alien who's landed on earth from Mars.

Frida glances at him and they both laugh.

'I don't think she saw you before. She's not used to me having company. Especially male company,' Frida says and immediately feels embarrassed. Why did she have to say that? As if Andrei was some kind of boyfriend or something.

'Her father?' Andrei asks.

What have you done? Now what are you going to tell him?

Frida moves her eyes away from the man and starts feeding Anne Sofie. The girl is still focused on Daniel's brother, as if on some level she knows that she's a relative of him. A thought occurs to Frida. Should she, for her daughter's sake, come clean? Shouldn't Anne Sofie be allowed to get to know her father's Romanian family?

'He's not around,' Frida says, not looking at Andrei.

At least that isn't a lie.

'Oh,' Andrei says.

Can she hear relief in his voice?

Finally, when Frida brings a spoonful of yogurt toward Anne Sofie's face, the girl takes her eyes away from Andrei.

'That was intense,' he says and gives another little laugh.

'Yeah,' Frida says and wonders whether he means the baby's stare or what happened between them just moments before.

There is a silence, broken only by the baby's munching. Frida has handed her the piece of rye bread, and she is trying to put it all into her mouth in one go, making the yogurt spread all over her face.

'You are a messy pup,' Frida says.

'She very pretty, like her mother,' Andrei says.

At that moment, Anne Sofie lets out a high-pitched shriek. Frida has stopped feeding her and she wants more.

'OK, baby girl,' she says and smiles at her daughter.

But her heart is beating so hard that her hand is shaking and she hears a faint vibration in her voice. She glances at Andrei from the corner of her eye to see if he's spotted the tremble in her body. And guesses that he is the cause of it.

She blows air out of her lungs when she sees Andrei is getting up.

'Sorry,' he says and disappears into the guest bedroom.

While she's finishing feeding Anne Sofie, Andrei is nowhere to be seen. Frida's mind is a whirlpool of conflicting thoughts.

While Andrei is quite similar in looks to Daniel, his personality is completely different. He seems quiet, yet his reactions just now revealed a passion that Daniel didn't possess. Daniel would never have tried to kiss her like Andrei did just now. Or was he about to do that? Perhaps Frida's mind is playing tricks on her. The way he reacted when she hugged him was not what she'd expected.

But, if she is right and he was about to touch her in that way, he's very different from Daniel. Andrei is more confident, and there is an intensity that she doesn't remember in Daniel. Frida finds these qualities very attractive. Her heart flutters even now when she thinks that Andrei is in the apartment, probably sitting in the room brooding over her. Or is he? Perhaps he has a wife and children at home in Romania and he was just being nice? Or he sleeps around?

If, however, he is free and interested in Frida in that way... Again, Frida's heart quickens in her chest. How would he react if he knew that his younger brother had been in love with Frida? That he fathered her daughter?

Frida isn't even certain how she feels about the family connection. It feels strange, but at the same time it feels right. But perhaps Frida is jumping ahead of everything here. Perhaps Andrei has no feelings toward her at all?

Besides, she hardly knows this man. She's sure he is Daniel's brother, but apart from that, how can she trust him? He could try to get information out of her by seducing her, couldn't he? And even without knowing Daniel's connection to her, he could still start digging into her father's past.

And what does Frida know about Andrei? She has only known the man for a matter of hours!

Frida wipes Anne Sofie's face and gives the girl a water beaker. The baby drinks thirstily and then gives a loud burp.

'Good girl!' Frida smiles at her daughter. 'Get down now?' She asks and the baby nods vigorously.

Frida sets the girl inside a large playpen in the lounge and surrounds her with soft toys and a crochet blanket that she knows the girl likes to suck at.

She finds Andrei sitting on the bed in the spare bedroom.

'You OK?'

He lifts his eyes toward Frida, which again sets in motion a jolt of desire inside her.

'Can you help me with Daniel?' Andrei asks.

'Of course,' Frida replies, although she has no idea what else she can tell him about his brother. Apart from the things she's not going to divulge. Not now, probably never.

She just can't.

CHAPTER FIFTEEN

B ack at the farm, I settle into the work again and it feels as if, returning to the little red cottage, I'm at home.

And then I meet her.

This year, there is no Florian, but an older man from Finland. He's even more quiet than the Romanian, and doesn't speak English, or Swedish. I'm disappointed, because I'm trying to learn more of both languages. I know I'll need to know both if I am to manage on my own in Sweden – or on the island.

This second summer in Åland is, at first, very lonely, so one Friday night in early June, before what the islanders call Midsommar, I accept an offer of a lift into the little town of Mariehamn from Mr Ulsson.

He is a kind man, unlike the farm manager, so I try to smile and even talk to him as often as I can. This day, Lars Olen is away somewhere and so I can accept this kind gesture from Mr Olsson without arousing the wrath *of the farm manager. I have told him I want to learn Swedish.*

Perhaps that is why Mr Ulsson tells me there is a library in the town. He drops me off outside and tells me he will come back in two hours.

Those two hours change my life.

She is hard to miss in the vast round building, filled with light. Long bookshelves jut out from the middle, where there is a desk, manned by two women. One of them, I learn later, is called Frida. She speaks fluent English and directs me to a section to the far right of the library. But I cannot concentrate on her words because her eyes are so beautiful. Or is it her face, which is framed by a mop of spiky, bright red hair? Her blue eyes are friendly, and her lips curl up at the corners.

'Shall I show you?' She asks with a wide smile.

I nod. It seems I've lost the ability to speak.

As the girl picks up a set of keys from the desk and walks around to a little, low gate that separates the hall from the reception, I take in her slim figure.

She's the loveliest thing I've ever seen.

'Where are you from?' The girl asks as we walk down a set of stairs and along one bookshelf, which ends at a tall window. Bright sunlight floods into the space and I see that there are similar windows with sofas in front of them all around the outer wall of the library.

'Romania,' I say and feel my face flush. I'm glad that I am walking behind her, and the girl hasn't turned around to see me blush like a little boy.

She leads me past another few bookcases, windows and sofas. I notice there are also desks with computer terminals, where some kids and some older people are sitting and staring at the screens. While others sit on the sofas, reading, or at tables and desks dotted around, talking in hushed tones with each other.

This place is heaven!

'What's your name?'

The girl has now turned around and is looking up at me. She's quite petite, but perfectly proportioned.

I'm filled with a sudden desire to lift her up into my arms and whisk her away. I shake my head and I feel a heat rising from my throat again.

'Umm, I ...'

Luckily, I manage not to blush this time.

The girl reaches her hand out and says, 'Frida.'

I take her hand and kiss the back of it. I didn't plan to do this, but it's something I've seen men do in old films, and it just seemed right.

But the gesture makes Frida giggle.

'My name is Daniel,' I manage to mutter.

'Well, you're a gentleman, Daniel' she says and pointing at the bookshelf, adds, 'You should find what you are looking for over here.'

I watch as Frida walks along the bookshelf toward the middle until I lose sight of her. My heart is beating so hard, I fear a gray-haired woman reading a large volume at a desk close to the bookshelf can hear it. I take a deep breath and start studying the volumes along the shelves.

CHAPTER SIXTEEN

W hen Ebba approaches the front desk, she sees a tall, dark-haired man standing in the middle of the waiting space. An officer had alerted her to a visitor wishing to talk to her about the death of Daniel Tamas. 'He says he's the boy's brother. He's only now been informed of the accident.'

That news intrigued Ebba enough to agree to see the young man herself.

'Hello, I'm the Police Chief. You wanted to talk to me?' Ebba asks in English.

'Andrei Tamas,' the man says.

He's very tall, almost as tall as Ebba herself. She also recognizes that he's very handsome, in a rugged sort of way. He's got strong arms and a wide chest. If she liked men, this is the type she'd go for, Ebba thinks, and she smiles to herself. Better not tell Jabulani about the visit. Her partner is intensely jealous, something that came as a bit of a surprise after they set up home together on the islands two months ago.

'Let's go to my office,' she says and leads the Romanian man through a long corridor.

Once seated opposite her, the man says nothing. He looks around Ebba's office, finally turning to face her. His dark eyes scrutinize Ebba, as if to assess her trustworthiness.

Ebba straightens her back.

'How can I help you?' She asks.

He's got exactly two minutes to come to the point, Ebba thinks, glancing at her police issue watch.

'I want to know what happen to my brother.'

'Didn't you get our report?'

'Yes. But I don't believe this accident.'

Ebba leans toward the man.

'Why not?'

'He keep a diary. And he write to us at home every week. Suddenly all stops. It does not make sense.'

The man is obviously still grieving, Ebba thinks and says softly, 'I know it must have come as a shock, but sadly, it is quite common on the islands to have an accident at sea. Especially if you are not used to the conditions. We believe his injury contributed to the sad events.'

Andrei Tamas shakes his head vigorously.

'This is wrong. Daniel was good fisherman, he had learned well here on the islands. It was his second summer!'

The man opposite Ebba gets up from his chair and puts both of his hands on Ebba's desk, leaning close to her face. 'I do not believe this was as you say, "accident". I think my brother was murdered by Russian.'

Ebba is silent for a moment, but the young man in front of her doesn't elaborate. An accusation of murder is a serious matter, but Ebba still thinks the man is exaggerating. But if he has a name ...

'There are many Russian tourists on these islands,' Ebba says eventually.

'He keep a diary,' Andrei says, as if he hasn't heard Ebba.

'Who?'

'My brother.'

'Right.'

Ebba is getting impatient and glances pointedly at her watch again. She gazes at the Romanian in front of her. His eyes are peeled and his face has a determined expression. He obviously doesn't have a name for the Russian he says he suspects of murder, otherwise he would have given it as soon as he came in. But then, something in the young man's demeanor makes Ebba change her mind.

He must still be in shock. If he only received the information about his brother last week, over a year after his death, it will be a fresh wound to him. Ebba is surprised it's taken so long to inform Daniel's family, but at the same time she knows that the bureaucracy between different countries' authorities sometimes causes unfathomable delays.

This young man, the grieving brother, obviously wants Ebba to do something, start to reinvestigate his brother's accident, but surely he must understand she can't do that? Perhaps it's a language issue. Is it the

Romanian's limited English that is making him appear so obtuse?

'He says he is good at rowing,' Andrei adds, quietly.

'I'm sure he was, but even the most skilful of seafarers can have accidents. And he couldn't use his leg, so perhaps that made a difference.'

Ebba recalls the case well, mainly because of the involvement of Alicia, her old schoolfriend and her stepfather. It's less common for a fisherman to drown these days, but there was absolutely no evidence of any other reason for the boy's death. He was an inexperienced boatman to boot. She is, however, not going to say this to the young man in front of her. It would only fuel his suspicions. But everything in the case pointed to a simple accident.

'Look, I understand you are upset,' Ebba says, leaning toward Andrei.

Seeing his expression harden even more, Ebba adds, 'You are grieving and looking for answers. That's understandable, especially as your brother was lost as sea so far away from home. But I can assure you, we did everything we could to find out what happened. It was a horrible accident. I'm so sorry for your loss.'

'But the diary,' Andrei insists.

Ebba sighs.

'OK, I'll read it. Do you have it with you?'

'No.'

Ebba rises from her desk and extends her hand toward Andrei.

'Why don't you drop it off and I will have a look.'

The young man stays put on his chair.

'You have it.'

Ebba sits back down.

'I'm sorry, I don't understand,' she says.

One more minute, she thinks.

'In letter I have from old Grigore Levandovschi say police have Daniel's things.'

'Ah, OK. Let me find out. I will inform you. Give the front desk your contact details and I'll see to it that you are notified when we have anything to tell you.'

Once again, Ebba gets up and offers her hand to the man.

This time the young man rises from his seat too but hangs his arms by his side.

'I will be here until I find out. I will not give up.'

There is an accusation in his voice. He keeps his eyes on Ebba for a minute longer than necessary before he turns on his heels and leaves.

His visit leaves Ebba with an uneasy feeling. She decides she cannot ignore what the young man had insinuated. Especially as he mentioned 'the Russian'. Surely this couldn't have anything to do with Dudnikov after all?

When Ebba had been the detective in charge of the investigation, she had found nothing to link the events to the internationally wanted criminal. But she wishes she'd been able to interview Dudnikov, especially after Alicia told her what the Swedish police had said. It still irks Ebba that she'd let him slip last winter.

She'd been so close.

CHAPTER SEVENTEEN

Hilda smooths down the red throw she's arranged at the foot of the bed in the attic. She's decided to put Leo in what she thinks to herself as the 'family room', which used to be Alicia's when she was a girl. It's also where she slept when she came back for holidays with her ex, Liam, and their son Stefan.

A sudden sense of loss and sadness fills Hilda when she thinks about her beautiful grandson, now forever gone. She sits down on the bed and takes a few deep breaths, trying to calm her heart, which has started beating fast. She succeeds in holding back the tears that prick the insides of her lids. Sighing, she gets up again and makes her way downstairs.

It's just gone twelve noon when she sees Alicia striding alongside the farm manager, Lars, in the field nearest to the house. Hilda watches them from the kitchen window and a sense of pride fills her chest. She cannot believe how quickly Alicia has stepped into Uffe's shoes. She appears to have learned everything about how to run the farm in just a few months. Although she wouldn't have dreamed of telling her daughter at the time, Hilda did have her doubts at the beginning, when she'd managed to convince Alicia to stay on the islands to look after Uffe's land. She wanted so much to have her daughter close to her, she would have told her anything to keep her on the islands instead of returning to Stockholm.

This calls for a little celebration.

Hilda opens the fridge door and pours a large glass of white wine for herself. She drinks it in two mouthfuls and fills it again.

She takes the glass and moves back to the window. But now she sees Alicia and Lars have stopped at the far end of the field. Alicia is moving her hands and speaking animatedly, while Lars stands in front of her with his arms crossed over his large belly.

Suddenly Hilda's daughter turns on her heels and starts walking fast toward the house. Hilda is startled and empties her glass quickly. She rinses it in the sink, making sure she removes the red lipstick smears from the rim. She hurries to get a dishcloth to dry and place it in the cabinet, and takes out a tumbler. She has just time to draw a glass of water from the faucet and bring it to her lips before Alicia storms into the house.

'What's up?' Hilda asks her daughter, who's pacing the kitchen floor.

'I can't believe it!' she says. 'Did you know anything about this?'

Alicia's eyes are alight, and her breath comes in and out in short bursts.

'About what?'

Alicia continues to take quick steps, moving from one end of the small dining area to the other.

'Sit down and have a coffee.'

Hilda tries to calm her daughter. A glass of the wine Hilda has just gulped down would probably be more suitable, or even a shot of vodka, but Hilda knows how Alicia feels about drinking during a working day.

'It'll calm you down and then you can tell me all about the problem,' she adds.

Alicia sighs but does as her mother asks.

'No coffee, I've already had three cups today,' she says while perching on her favorite stool in the corner, where the kitchen units end.

She lifts her eyes toward her mom and asks, 'How did Uffe get hold of the foreign labor he used on the farm?'

Hilda stares at Alicia for a moment, then turns and busies herself with coffee. Her heart starts beating hard again and she feels a dread creeping into her stomach and up to her chest.

'You know I wasn't involved in how Uffe ran the farm.'

Hilda turns on the percolator. 'Are you sure you won't have coffee?'

Straightening her back, she faces her daughter.

Alicia's eyes are boring into her, but Hilda decides she has to play it cool.

'What is it, darling? If you tell me all, I might be able to help you.'

Alicia looks down at her hands resting on her lap and shakes her head.

'Something isn't right. I knew Uffe paid them cash in hand, but Lars is being very cagey about how he found them and made all the arrangements.'

Hilda considers her daughter. From a young age, Alicia had a very strict, black and white idea of fairness. She remembers when she was around four, playing with her little friends in the sand on Nabben beach. It was a beautiful summer's day and Hilda had taken a picnic to the seashore, where she had found two mothers with their little ones from the nursery Alicia had started attending also enjoying the sunny weather. The children, two girls and a boy, were squatting, digging in the sand, when the boy accidentally sprayed sand into the eyes of one of the little girls. Hilda can't now remember what the boy was called, but the girl was Brit, who became Alicia's best friend. She can recall clearly the boy's sandy-colored hair, which was striking against his piercing dark eyes (his father was Spanish, she suddenly remembers).

Alicia demanded that the boy issue an apology to Brit and hug her as evidence of his repentance. Hilda and the two mothers watched as Alicia, standing tall with her hands on her hips, ordered the boy to comply. Glancing at the boy's mother – a pretty slightly built girl, originally from the outer archipelago and now living with her Spanish husband in Mariehamn – Hilda had been glad neither parent interfered. She knew Brit's mother of

course, they'd already met at the mother and baby classes
the council ran for new moms and was certain she would
find the whole episode amusing, but Hilda had been
worried about the reaction of the boy's mother.

As it turned out, the woman was a good sport and
didn't interfere. After the boy had hugged Brit, her mom
wiped away her tears, checked there was no sand in
Brit's eyes (Hilda wasn't convinced any had actually
reached the little girl's face) and told her to go back to
join her friends.

'You've got a future policewoman there,' Brit's
mother had said, nodding toward Alicia.

Hilda had smiled and lifted her cup of coffee from
the thermos to her lips to hide some of the pride she felt
for her little girl.

Later, of course, Alicia's strict moral code needed to
be carefully navigated. Just as Hilda is doing now.

'Mom?' Alicia asks, her face as serious as it had been
on that sunny day a hundred years ago.

'Sorry darling, miles away.'

Hilda takes Alicia's hands in hers and says, 'You
know I don't know the ins and outs of Uffe's farm affairs.
I wish I'd taken more notice, but I didn't.'

licia is about to press her mother when her phone rings. She walks out of the house and crosses the yard into her own home.

'Hello, you,' Patrick says, his tone soft.

Hearing his voice makes Alicia smile. Perhaps she is imagining that their relationship is changing.

'I miss you,' she says.

She hears Patrick take a deep intake of breath.

'Me too.'

'When can you come over? Next weekend?'

Alicia puts a strand of her hair behind her ear as she waits for Patrick's reply. She hates being the needy girl-friend, but with the difficulties over the farm and her mother's obtuse denial of any knowledge of how Uffe ran things, she feels very alone.

'What's up?' Patrick asks with a worried edge to his voice.

'Oh, nothing.'

Patrick gives a little laugh.

'You know I can't help you if you don't tell me the problem,' he says softly.

So, Alicia decides to tell him about what the farm manager has asked her to do. That he has a contact, a Russian, who can organize cheap – or cheaper – labor for the farm to work on the potato harvest.

'If we don't lift the potatoes soon, they will rot in the ground and we will lose our contract with Krisp.'

The company producing potato chips on the islands is Uffe's largest – only – client. The money they pay for the harvest sustains the farm. When Alicia agreed to take over the running of her stepdad's land a mere three months ago, she thought it wouldn't be too hard. She'd grown up on the farm and had often helped Uffe with the work when she was a girl.

She knew there were really just the two critical points – planting the potatoes and lifting them. There were two crops each year: the earlies and the main crop.

It's time for her first main harvest. The smaller spring yield, which went as well as it could, is about a third of the main crop. It's now important for her to show Krisp that Uffe's passing isn't going to make a difference to the farm's output.

'But you don't want to be involved with the Russians?'

'It's not that. I'm convinced there's more to it. Lars Olen – you know the farm manager? – was so evasive when I asked him where the Russians get the men from. We give them a place to sleep, but the Russians handle everything else. What if the Eastern Europeans don't get paid at all?'

'Hmm.'

Patrick doesn't sound in the least interested.

'Sorry if I'm boring you.'

'What? No, it's just I've had a work email about a story.'

Alicia gets an irrational desire to cut the conversation short but resists the temptation. It would only seem childish. Of course, Patrick is busy. They both are, and the reason why the relationship isn't exactly where Alicia would like it to be.

'No problem.'

'Don't get upset, Alicia. Let me look into this for you. I might find something that you can then throw in the farm manager's face. Would you like me to do that?'

'Sure.'

Try as she might, Alicia can't hide her irritation. 'You go and reply to that email.'

'I love you,' Patrick says.

'Love you too,' Alicia manages to reply, even though she really doesn't feel any kind of deep emotion toward Patrick at the moment.

As the line goes dead, Alicia sits down on her sofa. She follows a line of sailing boats making their way slowly toward Finland. The swing bridge over Sjoland canal must have just opened. It's the middle of July and the schools will be starting in August, so the holiday makers are slowly returning home to their ordinary lives. Alicia is looking forward to the quiet months on the islands, when, without the tourists, the population dwindles down. There are some hardy souls who still come over in the autumn, and even some for Christmas, but mostly the islanders will return to a sort of hibernation during the quiet time of the year.

Even Lars will be taking most of the winter off, going to live in his villa in Spain. Alicia wonders how on earth he has enough money to do this. But it's nothing to do with her, really. It's a relief to her not to have to pay him for the whole year anyway, so she should just be happy and not worry about things that have nothing to do with her.

CHAPTER NINETEEN

E bba is busy with a traffic accident for the next two days, so it's not until Thursday afternoon that she remembers the Romanian boy's diary. She calls her sergeant in and asks if they still have the case files at the station.

'No, they were sent to Helsinki, to the central records office,' says the older policeman who's become Ebba's unofficial right-hand man. Old Rönngren is from Finland himself, married to a woman from the islands. He investigated the case with Ebba.

'Do you recall there being a diary?' Ebba asks.

'Hmm.'

The older policeman is known for his reticence, so Ebba waits. She glances discreetly at the face of her cell. It's gone 4pm and she promised to be back early for Jabulani tonight.

Her girlfriend, who moved to the islands exactly eight weeks ago, has taken to life here in Åland surprisingly well. Dark-skinned and petite, she could have felt out of place in this small community filled with tall, blond, blue-eyed islanders. Stockholm, where Jabulani was born to South African parents, is far more multicultural. But even there she had some bad experiences.

Here in Mariehamn, she's thrown herself into the communal life. Tonight, for example, they are going to a dance class. Ebba is dreading it. Ebba has two left feet and has never even liked dancing. Her tall frame and long legs always seemed to get in the way of moving in a rhythmic way. When she was a teenager at school discos, she found she just couldn't match the other girls' movements, not even to the tracks of her favorite bands, Garbage and the Communards.

She's not as brave as Jabulani. She fears the session will be filled with heterosexual couples, and Jabulani will be the only one with dark skin. But, Ebba thinks, if her partner is willing to shake up the island folk, how can Ebba refuse?

'There were some books,' Rönngren says slowly, then rubbing his gray goatee beard, adds, 'One or two of them might have been diaries. I don't think anyone looked through his stuff in detail.'

Ebba makes a decision.

'OK. Contact the Helsinki Police and ask them to return the files and all other materials.'

Rönngren's untidy gray eyebrows shoot up and his bloodshot eyes peer at Ebba.

Ebba raises her hand, the palm facing the old policeman.

'This is not a reopening of the case. Tell them that a relative has come here and wants to have the victim's personal belongings. I don't want any rumors starting about the investigation. Make sure that's not going to happen. OK?'

'Yes, Ma'am.'

Rönngren nods and leaves Ebba.

The police chief grabs her phone and sends a message to Jabulani.

Leaving now.

CHAPTER TWENTY

P atrick enters the office late, and before he's
opened his computer, his editor shouts across
the open-plan office.

'I want to see you now.'

Patrick looks around himself as he quickly gets up –
the old man wasn't someone you wanted to leave waiting
– to see if any of the faces around him can reveal what's
going on. But everyone has their heads bent over their
keyboards. Were they studiously trying to ignore him?
It's rare that the editor wants to see anyone to tell them
good news, so Patrick picks up his cell, and walks
toward the large, glazed office at the end of the room.

'What are you working on?'

Jan Axelsson isn't looking at Patrick when he walks
into the 'inner sanctum', as the editor's fishbowl office is
called among the journalists who work for *Journalen*,
the largest broadsheet in Sweden.

'Hmm,' Patrick replies.

The truth is, he is working on several small projects,

none of which the editor would approve of. He calculates quickly that admitting to loose threads of stories is worse than appearing to have nothing on at all. It's better to be seen as lazy than stupid, he thinks, as he stands in front of the old man, biting his lower lip and rolling his phone around in his hands.

He wants to sit down on one of the plush jade-green sofas set into the corner of the office, where important guests and revered editors on the paper were often seen having a meeting with Axelsson. But his boss doesn't show any signs of asking him to take a seat.

Instead, Axelsson lifts his eyes from whatever he is reading on his large computer screen.

'We've been here before, Patrick.'

'I might have something brewing on Åland.'

As soon as the words leave his mouth, Patrick regrets them. What is the matter with him? Does he really want to ruin everything between himself and Alicia for good?

But it's too late. Axelsson leans back on his chair and lifts one eyebrow.

'Really? Tell me more.'

That same evening Patrick is sitting in his new, much smaller, apartment near Mariatorget metro station. He's facing the bright screen of his laptop, reading what he has written so far.

He's gathered together information he found online, his interview with the Polish boy, and the old diary. He'd almost forgotten that he'd kept it from the investigation he and Alicia were working on last year. What a stroke of luck he hadn't thrown it away during the move!

But he has a dilemma.

He wants to write the report in a way that won't hurt either the islands and Alicia's farm, or his own career. But if he even hints at what he now suspects – no knows – has been going on in Åland, it will more than damage Alicia's farming career. The information he has gathered will also sully her late stepfather's reputation, and that of many others on the islands. Alicia will never forgive him. Why would she?

There's also Frida and Anne-Sofie.

The name Alexander Dudnikov, whom he suspects is the mastermind behind the whole affair, is suspiciously absent from any of the material he's discovered. Which is a blessing in a way, since he is Frida's father and the little girl's grandfather. They are not in touch, but last year Frida inherited a fortune from her mother, who had worked all her life as a waitress at Hotel Arkipelag in the center of Mariehamn. How would she have amassed all that money if it had not come from Dudnikov? No doubt gained through highly illegal activities.

He can't write down his suspicions, however much he'd like to. And that will water down the whole article. And what will Axelsson say about that? He might not even print it if that's the case.

Patrick rakes his fingers through his hair and gets up.

He opens the balcony door. The air is fresh, even though he can't see the sea. He remembers his previous apartment and the uninterrupted view of Riddarfjärden.

Instead, he can see people hurrying toward the

entrance of the station below him, and others meeting friends, no doubt to have a drink or eat in the many bars and cafes in this part of town.

Patrick's new apartment isn't quite as close to the trendy places as his old apartment, owned by his ex-wife, Mia, but he was lucky to get somewhere in his beloved Söder. He can still walk to his favorite pizza place, and it's only a short subway ride from his work and the center of the city.

It's better than a place in the outer suburbs of Stockholm where crime is rife and cars are burned in the summer months out of sheer frustration.

The sun, which has disappeared behind the block of flats opposite him, is still warming the pavements below. Perhaps he should go for a walk around Mariatorget park, have a quick beer and then come back to his conundrum?

As he's getting ready to go out, he hears the rumble of a train. Being above the subway was the compromise he had to make, and the reason the rent is a little lower than it would otherwise be. He was worried when Alicia came over for the first time. She'd been used to seeing him in much more upscale surroundings, but she didn't seem to mind. She'd even mentioned that the place suited Patrick much better. He knew what she meant: she was happy that Mia was no longer in any way responsible for Patrick's living arrangements.

Apart from the apartment in Mariehamn.

Patrick agreed to keep it only because it was big enough for the girls to stay over with him. In Stockholm, he only had one spare room, which he uses as his office.

Now almost teenagers, Sara and Frederika hated sharing a room, and only stayed with him if their mother was away. But the other option of going to stay on the islands with their grandparents was even less attractive for the two teenage girls.

Patrick knows how oppressive Kurt and Beatrice Eriksson can be. They have all the money in the world to spoil their granddaughters, but it comes with a price. Strict rules on table manners, and on social interaction, as well as set bedtimes, are like a red flag to his eldest, Sara. And Frederika follows where Sara leads. Their loss and his gain, Patrick thinks and smiles.

He never saw eye to eye with his in-laws. He wasn't ambitious enough. Well, he'll show them!

Just as Patrick opens his door, he hears the buzz of his cell.

Alicia

Patrick bites the inside of his cheek as he gazes at Alicia's name across the screen. He wants to talk to her, but he just can't now. He hasn't worked out what he is going to do yet, and she will hear from his voice that he is hiding something.

He'll have to pretend he hadn't heard the phone. He puts the device on silent, places it in his breast pocket, and steps out of his apartment.

CHAPTER TWENTY-ONE

F rida gets out of her car and lifts Anne Sofie from her car seat.

'We're here,' she says to Andrei, whose eyes are staring at the large house in front of them.

Hilda's borders are at their best. A round flowerbed stands in the middle of the yard filled with several rose-bushes and edged with blue and white creeping Lobelia. The midday sun is high in the sky, and its rays caress the three-story white-clad house.

As Andrei gazes up at the perfect scene in front of him, Frida remembers when she first saw the house. She was sitting on the back of Stefan's moped, or the one he'd borrowed from his step-grandfather, Uffe. She had not gone inside the house, but she'd seen Alicia greet her son with a hug and then glance toward her, atop the motorcycle on the side of the road.

'It is very big.'

Andrei has stepped out onto the gravel path.

Frida gazes at him, standing next to her. She can feel the sorrow radiate from his body.

'This is where Daniel work?'

Frida nods.

'C'mon, let's go and see Alicia Ulsson. She's very nice.'

But instead of Alicia, it's Hilda who emerges from the main house.

Frida bites her lip. Why didn't she ring and arrange the meeting with Alicia? It was Andrei who insisted that she should not. He'd been acting weird since his visit to see the police chief.

'Gamme, Gamme!' Anne Sofie exclaims, stretching her fat little hands toward Hilda.

'What a lovely surprise!' Hilda says, taking the little girl from Frida.

'Are you glad to see *Gammelmormor,* darling?'

She coos to the little girl, rocking her back and forth. Then her eyes move from Frida to Andrei.

'Sorry, this is Andrei Tamas,' Frida says in English.

Andrei gives a little bow and extends his hand.

Hilda shakes it with her left hand, and they both laugh.

'She's getting heavy,' Hilda says in Swedish to Frida.

'Is Alicia around?' Frida asks, taking her daughter, who is kicking her legs and protesting, back into her own arms.

Hilda gives Andrei another glance. 'Sorry, you've just missed her. She's in town.'

'Oh,' Frida says.

'I'm not sure how long she'll be, but why don't you

come in and have some coffee? I've just baked a fresh batch of cinnamon rolls. I made some for the baby too, without the spices.'

Frida's face lights up in a smile. Hilda is famous for her baking and Anne Sofie loves her sweet buns.

'Why not! Thank you,' she says.

As they follow Hilda into the house, Andrei asks what's going on and Frida explains that Alicia is not here.

'Why we go inside?' Andrei asks. He stops at the steps to the house.

'You'll see,' Frida says and smiles.

'It's nice of you to introduce your new boyfriend,' Hilda says to Frida as she lowers a plate filled with delicious smelling buns on the table between them.

Probably because the word *pojkvän* sounds so very close to the English *boyfriend* Andrei lifts his eyes toward Frida. His eyebrows are high and there's a question mark in his eyes.

Frida shakes her head at him. She feels a heat rising to her cheeks and lowers her face down to her daughter, kissing her forehead. She hopes that neither Andrei, nor Hilda has noticed that she's blushing.

Anne Sofie is on her lap munching a bun, while Frida is holding a plastic beaker filled with milk in her hand. Frida is glad of the fuss her daughter made as they came inside. Her desire to be on the floor crawling is constant now, but Frida is glad of the distraction. Her breathing is getting back to normal,

and she hopes the blush has disappeared from her
face too.

'How about you sit on your own?'

Now the baby is concentrating on her snack, Frida
decides to place her in the highchair at the end of the
table.

'Hilda, Andrei is Daniel's brother,' Frida says, trying
to keep her voice level.

She fastens the harness over the girl and takes a
cinnamon bun.

Andrei too, has one on his plate, untouched.

'You should try it, they are wonderful. Still warm
from the oven.'

Switching to English, Frida smiles at Andrei and
then, turning to Hilda, says in Swedish, 'Very good, as
usual.'

'Daniel's brother?' Hilda repeats.

Her mouth is open, and she is staring from Andrei to
Frida.

'What is he doing here?' Hilda asks.

'We came to talk to Alicia, because she knew Daniel,
and ...'

'I don't mean here in Sjoland, I mean on the islands?'

'Ah,' Frida says.

'Yes?'

'He wants to know what happened to his brother.'

'An accident, that's was it was!' Hilda says, her voice
rising an octave or two.

'I know, that's what I told him,' Frida says, trying to
sound calm.

She's aware that Andrei's eyes are moving from her

to Hilda, as if by following the exchange between the two women, he might gauge what they are talking about. Frida is quite glad that Andrei doesn't understand any Swedish because Hilda is acting in a very strange way.

'Well, you haven't told him firmly enough, because you are here digging up old wounds. You know my husband is dead, don't you? He did absolutely nothing wrong. We were both shocked by what happened to poor Daniel. And I do not wish to be reminded of it.'

Suddenly, Anne Sofie lets out a cry. Her eyes, filled with large tears, are staring at Hilda. Her mouth is open revealing pieces of white bun.

Frida gets up quickly and takes the girl into her arms.

'Shh, shh, it's OK,' Frida says, trying to calm the baby down.

But her head keeps turning toward Hilda, as if she's some kind of monster.

'I'm sorry,' Hilda says and leaves the kitchen.

Frida can't understand what has just happened. It takes at least five minutes to calm Anne Sofie down. Eventually, Frida is able to pacify her with some formula from a bottle she keeps in her bag.

'There, there, darling girl,' she says speaking softly.

'She know something,' Andrei says when the three of them are back in the car and Frida is driving over the Sjoland swing bridge. The baby has fallen asleep in her seat. They've been driving in silence since leaving Hilda's house.

Hilda didn't come back to the kitchen, but Frida was

able to shout her thanks and goodbyes to her. She appeared briefly on top of the stairs when they were leaving.

'Sorry, I need to get a couple of bedrooms ready for visitors,' she said.

'Let Alicia know we came by.'

Frida saw Hilda's face change, harden almost, but the expression was gone as quickly as it had appeared.

'Of course.'

The older woman blew a kiss toward Anne Sofie, but the girl would still not smile at her.

'See you soon,' Hilda said and disappeared from view.

Hilda got upset over nothing, Frida now thinks. But she for one knew that grief could show itself at the most peculiar moments, so perhaps talking about Daniel, and the events of last summer, when Uffe was still alive and running the farm, had brought painful memories to the surface for her?

She glances at the man next to her.

'What do you mean?'

'This Hilda, she is having a secret about my brother.'

CHAPTER TWENTY-TWO

Hilda watches Frida drive away from the
house and turn onto the main road from the
attic bedroom window. She doesn't know
what to do. Should she tell Alicia about Dudnikov and
that poor boy? But knowing her daughter, she will not let
the matter lie. And Hilda cannot let Uffe's reputation be
tarnished. Besides, the little she knows about it all, might
not even be relevant.

Perhaps Dudnikov had nothing to do with it all.
What she has is all supposition. Uffe would never talk
about any of it with her, and all she knows is what she
overheard of a conversation in the kitchen between her
late husband and the farm manager, Lars Olen. She may
have misunderstood. She was herself in such a terrible
position with the Russian at the time, she may well have
got the wrong end of the stick.

Then when the poor boy died, and Uffe and Alicia
were so very upset by it all, Hilda didn't want to raise
any questions. Especially as they were both interviewed

by Ebba. Uffe was visibly shocked when the police-woman came around to talk to him. Hilda is absolutely certain that he gave her all the information he had. It was all above board. When the news came that the death was as a result of a fishing accident, Uffe was plainly relieved. Hilda remembers him sitting down on his chair in the lounge and placing his head between his hands.

Again, his behavior was natural in Hilda's mind. Before he was lost at sea, poor Daniel had had an accident on the farm, when one of the other temporary workers had reversed the tractor over his leg. The boy had simply been standing too close. Then when he'd gone fishing in the rowing boat with the small outboard motor that Uffe let the seasonal workers borrow, and drowned, Uffe felt responsible. Of course, he did. It was a relief that nothing strange had occurred. That the tragedy was just that – a tragedy. And that they could all move on. No one on the farm was at fault.

But what if...?

Hilda is brought back to the present, when she sees Alicia's car pull into the drive.

She sighs and hurries downstairs to greet her daughter.

Alicia is about to open the door to her small cottage. She's laden with shopping – she's been into town to get some provisions ready for her real dad's visit to the islands.

'Alicia, do you have time for a cup of coffee? I've made cinnamon buns.'

Her mother is standing on the other side of the yard, beyond the round border of vibrant dark-red rose bushes she's planted in the middle. Alicia remembers when Hilda bought the plants, years before. They were tiny, producing just a few roses each, and now you can barely see over the top of them.

'Sure, two minutes, I'll just put this stuff inside,' Alicia replies, thinking that her jeans were already getting a bit tight, and she should really not be accepting the offer, but Hilda's baking is just too tempting.

'Best yet,' Alicia smiles a few moments later when she bites into a still-warm bun.

But her mom seems distracted.

'Frida was here,' she says, sitting down opposite Alicia.

'Oh, I'm sorry I missed her. How was Anne Sofie?'

'Fine.'

Alicia finishes her cinnamon bun and takes a swig of coffee. Her mom loves the little girl above everything and usually makes a fuss of her whenever Frida visits or they babysit together. Afterward, she's full of stories about how clever the girl is, or what new word she's learned. It's unusual for Hilda not to elaborate on the baby's wellbeing.

'What's the matter, Mom?'

'Frida brought a young man with her.'

'Oh, really?'

'Yes, a Romanian boy, called Andrei,' Hilda says and gets up. 'More coffee?'

Her mom is standing with the pot in her hand, but Alicia shakes her head.

'What's wrong?'

Hilda doesn't answer straight away. Instead, she goes and places the coffee pot back on the percolator and stands with her back to Alicia. 'He's Daniel's brother.'

'Oh.'

'Frida and he seemed very close. Very close indeed.'

Alicia thinks for a moment. Did she know Daniel had siblings? She can't recall.

'What do you mean?' She asks her mom, who's behaving very oddly.

'I'm just saying,' she lifts her eyes toward Alicia, adding, 'At first I thought he was her new boyfriend.'

'Ah.'

Now Alicia understands. Hilda has become very protective of Frida, and particularly of little Anne Sofie.

'Daniel's brother isn't good enough for Frida, is that what you think?'

Alicia cannot but grin as she watches her mom feign surprise.

'No, not at all. He's very handsome, very handsome indeed, but ...'

'But what?'

'Don't you think it's odd that now Frida has all that money, and Daniel's baby, a good-looking elder brother suddenly emerges out of the woodwork?'

'You think he's not who he says he is? Surely not ...'

Hilda shrugs, lifting her arms out in a dramatic gesture.

'I don't know! I'm just looking out for Frida. She's all alone in this world with no one to protect her from gold-diggers.'

Alicia places her hand on her Mom's arm.

'I'm sure Frida wouldn't be fooled by someone like that. She must have evidence that this Andrei is truly who he says he is.'

'Well. Perhaps you're right. I just didn't like his style. He made Frida ask all sorts of questions about the Romanian boy, when she knows very well what happened.'

Now Alicia pricks up her ears.

'What kind of questions?'

'Oh, just how poor Daniel perished, if I knew anything more ... which I obviously don't.'

Here Hilda lowers her eyes and fiddles with the ear of her coffee cup.

For a moment, Alicia looks at her mom's hands, absent-mindedly admiring her perfectly painted nails. They are bright red, matching her lipstick. How does she manage to always be so immaculately turned out?

But then, her thoughts turn to Daniel. Does her mom know something more?

Alicia takes Hilda's hands into hers and says softly, as if trying not to frighten her, 'Is there something you're not telling me?'

Hilda straightens her back and pulls her hands away quickly.

'No, whatever makes you say that!'

CHAPTER TWENTY-THREE

F rida answers her cell on the first ring.

'Hello, I'm sorry I missed you,' Alicia says.

'Hi Alicia. We've just come back, but I'd like to talk to you. You see, I have Daniel's brother with me ...'

'Yes, Mom told me.'

'Ah. He'd like to talk to you about what happened to Daniel.'

Alicia is quiet for a moment. She can see from the small window facing the main house that her farm manager is on his way toward the cottage.

'Look, Frida, I've got to go, but can I come over tonight?'

As she ends the call, Alicia wonders what this Andrei thinks happened. A chill creeps down her spine when she thinks about her own awful suspicions in the days after she and Patrick saw the young man's body in the reeds around a small outcrop of rocks in the outer archipelago. They'd followed the police as reporters investigating the incident. She'd been shocked to realize that the boy was one of Uffe's farm laborers. She knows it upset her stepfather and Mom terribly too. Uffe was beside himself, because it had been his idea to let the farm hands use the fishing boat.

Her thoughts are interrupted by a confident knock on her front door.

'Come in, Lars,' Alicia shouts.

The farm manager walks in and Alicia asks him to sit at a chair she's placed next to her desk in the small office. The old milking parlor is divided into two. On one side there's Alicia's lounge and a bed in an alcove, plus a small bathroom with a shower. From her kitchen, which is in the middle of the building, there's a door to her lounge and the office. Her working space is about half the size of her living quarters on the other side of the oblong building. This space has hardly changed since it was Uffe's office. A fresh lick of paint, which Hilda insisted on, has been applied to the walls, and the wooden floor has been sanded and revarnished. Alicia has even kept Uffe's old heavy desk and left his faithful transistor radio in the corner. She doesn't listen to it anymore, but somehow having her late stepfather's things around her makes her feel better and gives her confidence in running the farm.

Not that she feels particularly self-assured today.

'We need to resolve the labor issue.' Lars says as if he knows exactly what Alicia is thinking.

Alicia nods. She's aware of what he wants to do, but she still has her doubts about the morality, let alone the legality, of what Lars is proposing.

'Everyone uses East European boys,' Lars says. His tone is soft now.

'I know,' Alicia says.

'Have you noticed that half of the field is in late bud? If this warm weather continues, they could be in flower by the weekend.'

Again, Alicia nods. She doesn't know what to do and she's ashamed to admit it to Lars of all people. She suspects that the farm manager doesn't think she is capable of taking care of Uffe's land. He has never said anything, and in the beginning, in the weeks after Uffe's death, the man had seemed pleased that the house and the farm wouldn't be sold off. But lately, Alicia can see in his eyes that he is disappointed in her.

'You know I'm off to Spain in a few weeks' time. If we can't get labor by then, I'm not sure what will happen.'

'I am aware,' Alicia says, more impatiently than she intended.

She looks at Lars, whose expression has changed from conciliatory to hurtful.

'The thing is, I've booked the flights and they can't be changed...'

'You will be able to go, don't worry,' Alicia replies.

She knows Lars has a place somewhere in Spain. He spends most of his winters there, taking many months off unpaid. She's often wondered how he can afford to do this, but Hilda says that he's living off his savings. *Must be some savings,* Alicia thinks absentmindedly.

'OK, this is what we will do. I will have another look at what we can get from the local labor exchange.'

Alicia's words are interrupted by Lars, who snorts loudly.

She lifts up her eyebrows and the farm manager gives an embarrassed cough.

'I'll call them now. If there's still no one available, you can go ahead and make arrangements with the Eastern Europeans.'

Lars's face lights up with a wide smile.

'Right you are, Miss Alicia.'

The farm manager steps out of the office in a hurry, leaving Alicia deflated. Why doesn't she have the courage to ask Lars what the exact arrangements are? Because she doesn't want to know. She is shirking responsibility, which is more than shameful.

She gets up quickly and goes to the door to call out to Lars, but he's disappeared around the side of the main house.

Back in her office, Alicia looks up the company name that Lars has given her once again. It's registered in Stockholm, and there is nothing unusual about it. She couldn't find any information on the three directors listed, but again, that is not unusual. She'd asked Lars if she could meet one of the directors, but he had nearly laughed in her face.

'I don't think they leave their office in the city. I've spoken with a woman, but she left last year, so I don't know who will be there this year. Probably a temporary secretary.'

That's when Alicia realized that Uffe's farm on the islands was indeed small fry for a labor agency in Sweden.

'Do you know if Uffe ever met anyone from there?' Alicia had asked.

The farm manager looked down at his hands and shook his head.

'Don't think so, Miss.'

Alicia sighed.

She wonders now if she should call Patrick to see if he's got anywhere with the details she's given him. But now, when the decision needs to be made in a hurry, she almost doesn't want to know.

She gazes at her cell, and sees that it's past 6pm. She decides to go and see Frida. She promised her mom that she would see if this Andrei is Daniel's brother, or an impostor. Although, truthfully, Alicia doesn't want anything to do with any of it.

The poor boy's death brought everything bad back to her mind: the loss of her own son, the break-up of her marriage, and the crazy affair with Patrick. Thinking of him, she remembers the last time they made love. It was more than two weeks previously, when Patrick had come to visit her for one night in the cottage. He'd been on the islands for just 48 hours, fitting Alicia in between seeing his daughters and his busy job in Stockholm. Since Mia, his ex, had decided to stay on the islands, Alicia and Patrick seemed to be sneaking around again, just as they had the summer Daniel died.

Alicia is certain everyone knows they're an item, but the influential Eriksson family hates seeing their precious daughter's estranged husband carrying on with a local woman. Because of their notoriety, wealth, and influence, any whiff of a scandal often spread in the newspapers and online blogs. It's a crazy situation, one that Alicia hates. But with the farm needing her constant supervision, it was equally difficult for her to tear herself away from the islands and go to see Patrick in Stockholm.

The love-making had been a hurried affair, and afterward Alicia had wondered if their relationship was strong enough to survive all the difficulties they faced. She understands that Patrick wants to keep the peace with the mighty Kurt Eriksson as well as Mia, for the sake of his daughters, but Alicia feels as if she is the one losing out.

As always.

Stop feeling sorry for yourself.

Alicia admonishes herself and locks the door to her cottage. She steps inside Hilda's kitchen and sees her mom sitting at the table with a glass of white wine in front of her. She goes to give her a hug.

'How are you doing?'

Hilda spots the car keys in her hand and nods toward them. 'You off somewhere?'

'To see Frida and this Andrei person.'

'Ah, of course.'

Her mom looks so sad and lonely, and for a moment, Alicia thinks she should ask her to come along. But knowing Hilda, she'd only dramatize the situation, so Alicia squeezes her mom's shoulder and says goodbye.

'I'll pop in later to let you know how it went,' she shouts from the door.

CHAPTER TWENTY-FOUR

'And there was no diary?'

Ebba glances up to look at Rönngren.

The older man shakes his head.

'Only the items you see there,' I'm afraid.

Ebba picks up some of the assorted bits and pieces, all bagged in clear plastic pouches and looks through them again. There's a bunch of keys, a book in English, *The Adventures of Huckleberry Finn*, and another in Swedish. A title Ebba doesn't recognize. She ignores the clothing, a hoodie and a pair of jeans plus some underwear, as well as the few toiletries. She picks up the cell phone. It's an old-fashioned pay-as-you-go Nokia phone. She recalls that they got very little information from it. Just a few texts sent to Frida and Alicia's late son, Stefan.

That was it.

She did find it strange that there were no calls going out or coming in, but she knew Daniel was short of money, so perhaps he kept the phone for emergencies only?

He hadn't even taken it out with him fishing on that fateful day. Of course, it had none of the features new phones had, so they couldn't even determine Daniel's movements in the days before his death. All you could basically do was make calls and send messages.

Ebba sighs as she sees how little is left of the Romanian boy. She thinks back to the brother, and his obvious anxiety. How is she going to tell him that the diary isn't there? And that this is all his beloved brother left behind?

The old policeman is looking at Ebba with obvious curiosity.

'The brother mentioned a diary, that's all,' she says and adds, 'Thank you, Rönngren. This is all I need.'

Ebba waits until the old policeman has closed the door to her office and goes behind her desk. She picks up her own cell, a new Galaxy as far removed from poor Daniel's phone as it is possible to get.

'Patrick, I need to talk to you about the Romanian boy's case. I'm sure you remember it. Daniel Tamas.'

Ebba hears the Swedish reporter cough at the other end. *Typical delay tactic*, she thinks.

'Yes?' He replies.

OK then, let's play it like this.

'I'm calling you because there is an item missing from the things recovered from Daniel's cottage in Sjoland.'

'Really?'

Now Ebba can hear some doubt in Patrick's voice.

'You wouldn't know anything about that, would you?'

'No, of course not!'

The man's denial is far too forcefully expressed. Ebba sighs.

'I seem to recall that I let you have a look at the items, together with Alicia, after the investigation. At that time, the diary was still there.'

There's a silence at the other end of the phone. But Ebba waits.

Finally, after several minutes, Patrick replies, 'Are you accusing me of something?'

'No, not at all, 'Ebba says.

The fact is that the diary isn't listed as one of the items stored in Helsinki, so Ebba really cannot bring any charges against anyone. Besides, none of it matters anyway because the diary didn't have any information in it. True, she remembers that there were sections in Romanian, which they hadn't been able to fully translate due to budget restrictions, apart from running them through an online program. But there was no relevant information indicating that the poor boy's death was anything except accidental.

Apart from the fact that Daniel's brother is on the warpath and wants the diary back. Thank goodness she didn't reveal its existence to the Romanian who came to see her.

'That's OK then.'

Patrick sounds distinctly relieved, and Ebba gets the feeling he knows something. But what can she do about it? She has no open case, no evidence on the existence of a diary, nothing.

'It was good talking with you,' Ebba says and ends the conversation.

When Patrick puts the phone down after his brief, but informative, conversation with Ebba Torstensson, he goes straight to his laptop and begins searching. He doesn't notice that the light has faded until he hears shouting on the street below. He's been working for over three hours, but he's got what he wanted. He leans back in his chair and rotates his shoulders to loosen up.

He's found more than he needs. Perhaps another visit to Husby suburb in the northern outskirts of Stockholm to interview the young man again? It will be difficult, almost impossible, but you never know he might get lucky.

He dials the number of a policeman friend at the Stockholm Crime Unit, but there's no answer. Patrick realizes it's gone ten o'clock at night and he hasn't had anything to eat. Pizza for all his efforts, he thinks, and gets out of the apartment.

As he walks along the street, which is now filled with young revellers, spilling out of the bars, he thinks to himself that he has a good story on his hands – one that will save his career on the paper.

But can he submit it? What will it cost him if he does?

CHAPTER TWENTY-FIVE

W ith the help of Mr Olsson, I become a regular at the Mariehamn Library.

I feel very lucky to discover that Frida works at the weekends, which this year on the island, I too have as free time. It seems as if coming back for a second year, the farm manager and especially Mr Olsson and his glamorous wife trust me to do the work during weekdays.

Of course, there are times when the potatoes need to be lifted seven days a week, especially if there is rain coming, but I don't mind that. This summer, though, the skies have been clear and the rain has come during the night.

'Gods are smiling on us,' Mr Ulsson told me just yesterday.

I make sure I am in the library when it opens on both Saturday and Sunday. Spending so much time there is no problem. It is a beautiful building filled with light and books. How can anyone not love the place?

The bicycle has become my main form of transport into town. As Lars Olen told me, it takes only twenty minutes to cycle along the seashore to the small town.

As the weeks go by, I become more courageous, and instead of just nodding to Frida and asking how she is, I begin to have longer, hushed, conversations with her. On my fifth visit, when on a Saturday morning I find her alone at the desk, I pluck up the courage to ask her if she'd like to go for a coffee with me.

Frida cocks her head to one side, as if thinking about my proposition, and I hold my breath.

'OK, meet me here at 12,' she says after what to me seems like several minutes.

Frida gives me a smile and moves her eyes back to the large screen at the desk.

'See you later,' I say, too loudly, because a couple of older women turn their heads and look at me. Frida glances toward the two women and returns her eyes to me.

We grin at each other.

That day I can't concentrate on my Swedish course book, which I read each time I come to the library. Frida has told me that I can borrow the book, but I have declined. I prefer coming into this beautiful building instead of reading alone in the cottage in Sjoland.

I don't tell Frida that I'm pulled back by the prospect of seeing her and the wild red hair and those blue eyes. I often position myself so that I can have a good view of the desk where Frida works, but I try not to stare at her too much. I worry that in a place, where there aren't many other people coming and going, and most sit for hours reading, like I do, my interest in Frida would be noticed. So I try to be discreet and not scare her away.

But now, she's agreed to go for a coffee with me!

I cannot believe my luck. I glance at my watch and see that it's just gone ten o'clock. I have two long hours to wait. I try to concentrate on the text in my book and write down the phrases:

Det regnar idag – It's raining today

Solen skiner alltid I Karlstad – The sun always shines in Karlstad

Det blir molnigt imorgon – It's going to be cloudy tomorrow

Igår var vädret bra – The weather was fine yesterday

I repeat the words over and over, muttering to myself. I write them down on a pad that I found in the cottage, but my mind isn't working today. I just cannot focus on the work.

Finally, it's five to twelve and I pack my bag, return the Swedish language course book to its place on the shelf and walk – trying to slow down my gait – toward the central desk.

Frida is nowhere to be seen, but as I approach the reception area, she comes out of another door to the side.

'Ready?' She says, and I nod.

We walk side by side into the bright sunshine. Frida seems to know where to go, which is just as well, because I have not been to a cafe in town yet.

I try not to spend any of the little money Lars Olen gives me at the end of each week. I am saving toward when I am free to work for myself. Suddenly panic rises in me when I realize that I should know where to go. I had asked the girl for a coffee after all. I look at Frida who is walking next to me.

She smiles at me and asks, 'Do you like pizza?'

We go inside a small restaurant and Frida asks if I want to share a pizza and I nod and let her choose. The prices of the food shock me, but I have my wallet with me so I can pay, even if it will make a big dent in my savings.

When we are sitting opposite each other, drinking coke out of plastic cups, Frida says, 'You're not saying much.'

Her eyes are wrinkled at the corners and she has her head cocked.

'My English is not so good,' I say and add in Swedish, 'Men jag lär mig svenska – I'm learning Swedish.'

'I know,' Frida replies in English and gives a little laugh. I am embarrassed. Of course, she remembers when I first came in and asked her about the language books.

She turns her head and looks at the counter, where she ordered a ham and pineapple pizza. Behind it, a man dressed in a white apron and a chef's hat uses a large spatula to place the food inside an oven with a gaping fiery mouth.

Perhaps I could learn how to make pizza?

There is a silence while I try madly to think of what to say next. But I am paralyzed by being so close to Frida. Her scent of strawberries and something else – lemons – is intoxicating.

'So, do you like it here?' Frida suddenly asks. Her eyes are on me, and I have to swallow before I reply.

'Yes, but ...'

I want to tell Frida about the Russians and how I can't wait to pay back my debt to them so that I can have my passport back and start deciding what I want to do myself. But everybody keeps telling me not to talk, and that if the Russians find out you've blabbered, they will add thousands and thousands to your debt. I keep thinking about the leather bag one of the men had on the bus from Romania. I've not seen the bag since, but I'm sure if I did, I could pinch my passport back. According to my calculations, two summers on the island and a winter in Stockholm must be enough to pay off the travel costs.

The cash I get is so little, compared to what I have seen people are paid in the newspapers. One advert for cleaners in Stockholm had the salary at ten times what I am paid. I don't contribute toward accommodation, but one room in an apartment, miles away from where we work, shared by several men, cannot be that much. And Lars Olen told me that the cottage in Sjoland is part of the 'package' for any of the summer laborers. Perhaps that costs a lot. It's certainly luxurious compared to the place in Stockholm.

I realize I've been deep inside my own thoughts and that I should be talking with Frida now I have her here. But I can't think of anything to say.

Luckily, Frida is the talkative kind.

'But what?' She asks, leaning over the table, coming closer to me.

I study her face. Her features are so open and friendly that I nearly crumble and tell her everything.

'It's complicated.'

Just then, a girl with long brown hair places a pizza on the table between us. She gives us a plate each and nods to the cutlery in a tin next to the kitchen.

'Help yourself to sauces too,' she says in English.

'I'll go,' I say.

I'm relieved that the conversation has been interrupted. I know nothing good will come out of telling Frida about my life.

CHAPTER TWENTY-SIX

Every time Alicia enters Frida's new apartment, she is faced by another dilemma. All of what she sees has been bought with money made by Alexander Dudnikov. The Russian, who as far as Alicia knows, is a criminal. A loan shark who frightened Hilda and instigated the downfall of her little fashion boutique in town. Goodness knows what else that man has on his conscience.

Last year, Alicia's old schoolfriend, Ebba, the police chief on the islands, wanted to question the Russian, but he left the islands on a private plane before she had a chance. Since then, thank God, none of them had heard anything about Dudnikov.

Long may that last, Alicia now thinks.

Although Dudnikov is Frida's father, she never wants to set eyes on the frightening man again. Luckily Frida doesn't know about her father's criminal background. Alicia has managed to keep it from her, to protect both Frida and Anne Sofie. How would depriving Frida and the little baby of their secure future help anyone? Besides, even though she has proof that Dudnikov is a wanted man, she cannot say for certain that the money he gave over the years to Sirpa Anttila, Frida's mom, was illegally earned.

But Alicia isn't stupid, and neither is Frida. She knows that if the girl heard even a whiff of what Alicia knows, she would refuse to use any more of the money.

The woman at the door looks younger than Andrei imagined. She has long, blonde hair, caught up in a low ponytail. Her eyes are blue and she's wearing almost no makeup. She is older, but Andrei can see that she's beautiful.

Are these islands full of blonde beauties?

'Hello, I'm Alicia, you must be ..?'

'Good evening. My name is Andrei Tamas.'

He extends his hand toward the woman, but she just smiles.

'Can I come in?'

The woman looks past Andrei toward the kitchen where Frida is feeding her child.

'Yes,' Andrei says simply and lets Alicia pass him over the doorstep.

The two women hug and start speaking the incomprehensible language that Andrei knows is Swedish. Alicia's arrival has disrupted the little girl, and she begins to fuss with the bottle, so Frida gets up and takes the baby to her room.

Andrei sits in the chair vacated by Frida and examines Alicia's face.

The woman is smiling at him.

'You are Daniel's older brother, is that right?'

Andrei nods.

'You know him?'

Now the woman's smile fades and she looks down at her hands on her lap.

'Not really. I met him just once on my stepfather's farm.'

'This is Uffe Ulsson?'

Alicia lifts her eyes at Andrei, and he sees that there is a sadness in them. She nods once.

'My late stepfather.'

'Can I talk with him? I need to know what happen to my brother.'

Andrei believes that as well as the woman they met at the farm, Hilda, this daughter, and her father Uffe know more about his brother's death than they are saying. And he is determined to find the truth.

The woman in front of him sighs. Her face seems to be crumbling and suddenly Andrei realizes that she is about to cry. He panics. What did he say to upset her so?

At that moment, Frida comes back into the kitchen.

'At last, she's asleep,' she says and goes over to the large steel refrigerator.

'Would anyone like a drink? Beer or wine, Alicia? Andrei?'

When Frida turns around, she notices that Alicia is sitting quietly, not looking at either of them. She seems to be deep in thought, or fighting the tears that Andrei saw pooling in her eyes.

Andrei gets up and takes the few steps up to the kitchen counter. He says softly to Frida, 'I do not know what I say. But she is sad now?'

Frida stares at Andrei for a moment and then kneels in front of Alicia, speaking to her in Swedish. After a few moments, she steps back to the kitchen cabinets where Andrei is still standing, feeling hopeless.

He's never understood how women can change from being completely normal to tears in their eyes. His sister Maria is the same – just one wrong word from Andrei about the food she's dished up, or about her dress, can set her off in either a fit of rage or floods of tears.

'Her stepfather died a few months ago,' Frida says.

'Uffe Ullsson?' Andrei asks. Involuntarily, he puts his hand over his mouth. He's horrified. How did he not know that the owner of the farm where Daniel worked had died too?

'How?' He asks, but when he sees Frida's face, he understands that this is not a subject he should be talking about.

Nevertheless, Frida whispers a short reply, 'Heart attack.'

Alicia feels stupid. How can she still not talk about Uffe without dissolving into an emotional heap? She gazes at Frida and Daniel's brother as they whisper to each other a few steps away from her.

'It's OK,' she says out loud in English. 'I'd love a glass of wine. Just a small one, I'm driving.'

Frida turns around with a wide smile on her lips.

Andrei, too, faces her. His expression is a little softer now, the anger she saw before has faded.

'I'm sorry about Mr Ulsson,' he says simply, as he returns to the table, holding a bottle of beer in his hand.

'Don't worry. You didn't know,' Alicia says and adds, 'Why did you want to talk to my stepfather?'

Andrei hesitates. His eyes darken when he replies, 'I do not believe this accident. My brother was very good with boat. He did not have accident.'

Alicia gazes at Frida, who shrugs her shoulders as she too settles herself at the kitchen table.

'But the police ...' Alicia starts.

'I have talk to policewoman. She tells lies.' Andrei interrupts her.

'Who?'

Andrei brings out a piece of crumpled paper from his back pocket and sets it on the table. He points at a line, where in a formal-looking letter, all written in Romanian, Alicia spots the Åland police chief's name.

'Ebba would not lie,' she says more forcefully than she intended.

'I'm sure that's not what Andrei meant,' Frida says in a conciliatory tone. Glancing sideways at Andrei, who's sitting close to her, their bodies nearly touching, she continues, 'Andrei has some information. Daniel wrote home regularly, until ...'

'What information?'

Without understanding why, Alicia feels a cold shiver run through her.

Alicia stares at the bunch of letters that Andrei has handed to her. The name and address on the top of the envelope is in a childlike handwriting. Alicia glances at Andrei before opening one of the envelopes and taking out four pieces of paper. The man nods his head encouragingly.

'These are in Romanian,' she says, lifting her eyes up to the two young people sitting opposite her.

Andrei begins to say something but stops when Frida puts a hand on his arm.

'Andrei has translated some of them to me. Daniel talks a lot about Uffe and the farm in them, and in one,' Frida stops and picks up the pile of letters.

'Which one was it?' She asks Andrei, who shifts through them and finds one with several stamps.

'Here,' he says and hands it to Frida.

But the girl gives the letter back to Andrei and says, 'You read it in English like you did before?'

Andrei takes the pieces of lined paper out of the small envelope. For a moment, he holds the sheets in his hands and stares at them.

'It's OK, take your time,' Alicia says.

She can see how difficult all of this is for the young man. If there is one thing she understands, it's grief.

With a shaking hand, Andrei picks up the first sheet and begins to read, in English. At times, he stammers, but Alicia understands enough to see why Andrei is suspicious of the circumstances surrounding Daniel's demise.

Dear Brother,

This island is beautiful, as are the people living here! All blonde and blue-eyed, you've never seen anything like them. And they are nice, almost all, at least. I have friends too, Stefan who lives in London but comes and stays here in the summer and Frida. They are good to me and we have fun on Sundays when I don't have to work on the farm.

Today I went fishing. It's amazing how easy it is to get food out of the ocean. Uffe (that's the owner of the farm where I work) has given me a boat and fishing rod to use, but usually I get more fish with a net. But for that you need two people so if I go out on my own (this I usually do), I use the rod and some worms that Uffe has shown me how to use. I love being at sea on the boat and go out most nights.

I must tell you about the white nights!

It doesn't get dark at all during the summer. Can you believe that? The sun barely dips below the horizon before it gets up again. The fish, too, stay awake so night-time is a good time to try to catch them. And catch I do! This is why I can send you so much more money in the summer because of the fish. I eat a whole fish sometimes for supper instead of buying expensive food in the shop. I am clever, yes?

How are my siblings? Is Maria still as grumpy as she was when I left? How about Mihai, is he any help to you on the farm? Send them my love. As soon as the Russian lets me, I'll come and see you all!

Your loving brother,
Daniel

Andrei puts the pieces of paper back in the envelope.

'Can I see the letter?'

Andrei looks up in surprise, but hands Alicia the envelope.

Alicia scans the foreign text but can't see a name. She puts her hand out for the rest of the pile of letters.

'May I?'

Andrei nods.

Before she opens any of the envelopes, Frida gets up and comes to sit next to her.

'There's no name in any of the letters,' she says in Swedish.

Her eyes are serious as she gazes at Alicia.

But Alicia has to see for herself. Opening up all the envelopes, with panic rising in her throat, she tries hard not to tear at the papers as she looks for the name that she suspects might be there. Surely it has to be the same man? How many Russians are there on the islands?

'Do you know this Russian's name?' She asks Andrei.

The young man shakes his head.

'No. He arrange for Daniel to work here. And in Stockholm during the winter. But my brother like it better here. He say that the city was cold and damp and that they worked all night and day with no sleeping.'

Alicia's breath catches in her throat and fear creeps up through her spine.

'Could it be?' She says almost to herself, but Andrei sees that there is something she knows and pounces on her.

'What? Tell me!'

'When you say this Russian arranged the work for Daniel, what do you mean?'

Andrei tells Alicia that each spring, the Russian would come to the village and tell stories of the riches that awaited anyone who wanted to work hard in the Scandinavian countries.

'"We are European now, so we can work without any permits. All you need is the contacts," he say. And Daniel wanted to be rich. He wanted to help the farm.'

Andrei's head is bent over the table and Alicia can hardly hear his words when he continues, 'I let him go. A big mistake. But he wanted to... And we have so little money after father and mother dead. Three mouths better than four.'

There were no tears in Andrei's eyes, but the sadness emanated from his whole being as he lifted his head to look at the two women sitting opposite him. Then his face hardened.

'But you can see Daniel can take fish from sea. He did all the time. How he suddenly drown? It's not possible!'

Alicia doesn't say anything. She knows that Ebba would not have left any stone unturned when it came to Daniel's death. She's certain that the boy had a terrible accident at sea.

He should never have gone out on his own with a heavy cast on his leg. He was also on pain medication so his reactions would have been slower than usual.

But she doesn't want to say this to Andrei now. He will simply not accept it. She is also more worried about the circumstances under which Daniel was brought to the islands.

And the arrangements made with his stepfather.

'Why did he say in his letter that he needed the Russian's permission to come home to visit you?' Alicia asks Andrei instead.

While she waits for a reply, she glances sideways at Frida. Did the girl understand what she suspects?

Andrei shrugs his shoulders.

'He arrange the bus to here and the work. And holiday, I think.'

'And the pay? Did he also pay Daniel?'

Andrei shakes his head.

'I do not know. This is why I need diary.'

'A diary?' Frida asks before Alicia has time to.

Alicia cannot remember a mention of a diary while Daniel's death was investigated. She's sure Ebba would have mentioned it if they'd found such a thing.

'Yes. Daniel say in his letter he write diary. In Romanian, English and Swedish. He learning languages. This is what I want to ask you and your mother. Do you find it?'

CHAPTER TWENTY-EIGHT

J ust as she's about to start the car engine outside Frida's apartment, her cell buzzes.

She's relieved to find that it's Liam calling.

After their usual hellos and talk about weather – it's raining again in London – Alicia cannot help but tell Liam about Andrei and her problems with the farm.

'Liam, I'm in such a quandary!'

Alicia is leaning too much on Liam, she knows it. She feels guilty about their – sometimes late-night – phone conversations, and she hopes Liam doesn't think that this means she's about to give up her life on the islands and move back to London to be with him.

But she cannot stop calling and messaging him. Running the farm is much lonelier than she had imagined. She'd expected to more or less leave it all to Lars. He'd been doing it for decades, after all. But she now realizes that the way Lars wants to run the place isn't what she has in mind. This problem with labor is threatening to drive a huge gulf between them. What he wants to do is something she cannot even contemplate.

She can hear that Liam is worried by what she has said. He takes a long time to reply and when he does, his words are measured, and his voice has a serious tone to it.

'I think you need to be very careful now.'

'I agree. With Daniel's brother firing all sorts of accusations about, I'm not sure I can take it anymore. Can you imagine what he would do if he knew what I learned last year about Alexander Dudnikov?'

'What did you find out?'

'Firstly, he more of less bankrupted Hilda. I know Mom's fashion boutique in the center of Mariehamn never made any money, having seen her accounts by chance when looking after the shop one day. But Dudnikov took advantage of her vulnerable position by first making large purchases in the shop and lulling Mom into a false sense of security, and then offering her a loan. With that, he stopped coming to the shop unless it was to intimidate her. Dudnikov then increased the interest on the debt, so that it became impossible for her to pay it off. If it hadn't been for Uffe selling some of his land, Mom would never have got rid of the Russian.'

'Oh, goodness, I'd forgotten all this.'

'I know, but thing is, while I was with *Ålandsbladet*, I found out that Dudnikov has a criminal record in Stockholm and is on the run from the police. Apparently, he'd been convicted for extortion, with suspicions of money laundering and people trafficking, although they didn't have enough evidence to get him on those two more serious charges.'

'And what's your fear? That Dudnikov is the Russian mentioned in Daniel's letters? Surely there are more Russians on the islands than just this Dudnikov?'

Alicia is quiet for a moment. Liam is right. She is probably overreacting. She has to take time to think and not jump to conclusions. But she has to air all her doubts.

'Yes, there are, but how suspicious is it that Daniel needed permission from a Russian to go back home? Or that Dudnikov was here intimidating all and sundry around the same time? Or that the same man is suspected of people trafficking in Sweden? And now Lars wants me to employ more East European labor!'

Alicia feels close to tears. But she needs to control herself.

'You need to go with your gut instincts here. If it feels wrong for you, you have to tell Lars.'

Liam's voice is so calm, it makes Alicia, too, feel more settled.

'I know,' she replies simply. 'The thing is, I am even beginning to suspect my mom knows more about all this than she's letting on. It's just such a mess!'

There is another brief silence on the line.

'Look, Alicia, would you like me to come over? I have lots of leave that I've just not taken in the last year ...'

Alicia doesn't immediately reply. How wonderful it would be just to lean her head against Liam's chest and let him tell her everything will be alright. But she knows that their marriage is over and asking him to come and help her now would only indicate to him that she was thinking of giving up and returning to London. And she'll never do that.

'No, don't worry, I can do this. I'm fine.'

Liam thinks that Alicia is far from fine. But he doesn't want to undermine her.

'I know you can do it! I've said so many times. But sometimes you need help. And it's never wrong to ask for it, if you need it. I could come over, talk it all through with you, Lars, Andrei, and even your mom,' here Liam gives what he hopes is a nonchalant little laugh, 'and try to find out what is really going on. Or just be there to support you ...'

'You're so kind.'

Alicia interrupts Liam and her words deflate his mood like a balloon popped with the tip of a thin pin.

'OK,' he says.

'Don't be like that. I'm a big girl, remember? And quite stubborn with it.'

Now Liam can hear a smile in Alicia's voice.

'Don't I know it!'

Liam disconnects the call and puts his cell down. He goes over to his laptop and logs onto the hospital's staff site. He checks his calendar and shifts a few things around. He writes a couple of emails and goes back to his browser to find the Finnair site. He hates flying but needs must.

CHAPTER TWENTY-NINE

Andrei is quiet all evening after Alicia's visit.
Frida can tell he is brooding over the diary and over the facts of Daniel's death, but she can't talk to him about it. For some reason, which she doesn't really understand herself, she just can't tell Andrei about Anne Sofie's real paternity.

Not that Andrei has even asked.

And now he doesn't even mention Daniel, or the diary, or his brother's accident.

Frida thinks about the routine they've settled into. In the mornings, when the baby wakes up, Andrei also makes an appearance and sets out the breakfast for them while Frida feeds the little girl. Then Andrei plays with Anne Sofie while Frida takes a shower and gets dressed.

Frida hasn't realized what a difference having another pair of hands makes, especially now that Anne Sofie is becoming more and more mobile. She's on the cusp of walking and protests when either of them tries to put her down in her playpen. A few weeks ago, the baby happily sat there and played while she was in the shower.

But now, with Andrei there, Frida has more time to herself. Slowly, she's become more confident about leaving Anne Sofie with him.

He is the little girl's uncle after all.

During the evenings they talk. Andrei tells Frida about the farm, his brother and sister. He seems to love them all equally. Frida feels a pang of jealousy when she sees in his eyes how much he misses his village and his animals. But Frida also hears how little the family in Romania have.

They live in a simple farm cottage, where Andrei and his brother share a room. His sister sleeps in the small living room off the kitchen. Andrei's sister Maria dreams of a dishwasher and an electric washing machine. They have an old tractor, but Andrei has just bought some expensive milking equipment with a state loan. It makes their daily life more difficult, but he hopes in years to come, with an increased milk yield they will be better off.

Frida can't even imagine a life like the one Andrei is describing. What can he think of her and her luxurious apartment, with a beautiful sea view and a courtyard just for Anne Sofie to play in?

At the same time, Frida can hear the love in Andrei's description of his farm and family. Especially when he speaks about his little brother, who doesn't seem to be a natural farmer. To Frida he sounds a little like Daniel – a dreamer.

'Mihai is not very good at farm work. He does not like it,' Andrei laughs. 'But he does this for me.'

Frida is fighting tears when she thinks about Mihai.

'Do you have pictures?' She asks.

Andrei shows her images of the farm, his brother, and sister on his phone. Mihai is indeed almost a spitting image of Daniel, something that brings a lump to Frida's throat. His sister, however, is a real beauty. She is dark like Andrei, with high cheekbones and large brown eyes.

'Your sister is gorgeous!'

Andrei smiles fondly at the image on his cell.

'Yes.'

'How much younger is she?'

'Oh, eleven years.'

Frida thinks this explains a lot. Andrei must have looked after his siblings when he was a child and that's why he's so good with Anne Sofie.

Andrei has invented a new game with her. He tickles her and then moves away, and she has to crawl to him. Frida feels such happiness at the sight of her little girl's sparkling eyes gazing up at Andrei when she finally reaches him and then squeals in delight at a new tickling session.

Andrei is so gentle with Anne Sofie and seems to know exactly how to handle her. Not too rough, but confident enough for the little girl to feel safe and secure.

Now sitting on the sofa, with beers on the coffee table in front of them, Frida thinks back on the days they've spent together and realizes it's been nearly a week. She can't but wonder what Andrei's plans are.

'So,' she starts, but at that moment, Andrei leans across and kisses her lips.

His move takes her by such surprise that at first, she pushes herself away from him.

'Sorry,' Andrei says. He shifts along the sofa and brushes his hair back with his hands.

Frida's heart is beating so hard she can hear the thuds in her ears.

'No, don't be sorry,' she says and moves to sit next to Andrei.

He looks down at her and she puts her hand on the back of his head and pulls him toward her.

His lips are soft, and at first, they kiss tentatively, but soon Andrei's tongue enters her mouth. Frida's mind goes blank. All she wants is to continue kissing Andrei forever. But suddenly Andrei pulls away.

'I like you very much.'

'I know,' Frida smiles. The next moment, his face is close to Frida's again and his mouth is on hers. His fingers touch the nape of her neck, pulling her in, while his lips, tasting so wonderful, so full, and so hungry are pressing against her own.

Continuing to kiss her, Andrei gets up and pulls Frida away from the sofa and toward the hallway. One of his hands is now on the small of her back, while the other is on her hair. Frida knows she needs to stop this, but her whole body wants to keep kissing this wonderful man. She finds her hands are around his neck and she has a sense of falling backward as the desire in her body rises, and rises, and rises.

But before she has time to do anything, Andrei lifts her across his haunches with his strong arms. They kiss for what seems like forever until Frida, panting, pushes herself back.

'Let's go to my bedroom?'

CHAPTER THIRTY

The next morning, when Frida comes back to her apartment from dropping off Anne Sofie at nursery, she finds Andrei sitting at the kitchen table, nursing a beer. It's just gone eight thirty in the morning.

'You OK?'

'No,' he says, turning his large eyes toward Frida.

His hair is dishevelled and his chin and the skin above his upper lip is covered in a dark stubble.

Frida tries to ignore how handsome he looks in a tight T-shirt with a white Nike logo just next to his left shoulder.

'Have you had breakfast?'

Frida immediately regrets her words as she gazes at Andrei. She's turning into Hilda the way she's feeding her house guest! But he seems constantly hungry.

That's what motherhood does to you!

She grabs a beer out of the refrigerator, as if to prove to herself that she's not too old, or set in her motherly ways, to drink alcohol early in the morning. She seats herself opposite Andrei and opens the top of the bottle with a twist of her hand.

But the guy ignores the gesture, and the fact that Frida is drinking on a weekday morning. His eyes meet hers and he shakes his head slowly.

'Well, you don't have to, but I could make you an omelet?'

Andrei reaches out and takes one of Frida's hands. He kisses the palm, burying his face in it.

'You are beautiful, and kind, and ...'

Andrei's words are spoken into her hand.

Frida is suddenly taken aback. The heat of Andrei's breathing burns into her hand, and she begins to feel warmth rise up along her spine and into her chest. The hot stream of desire which he had awakened in her last night, returns. She lowers her eyes, when Andrei takes hold of her other hand.

They haven't talked about the night before, and she still feels awkward about it. Not about the lovemaking, that was wonderful, but about the secret she is keeping from Andrei. She knows she has to tell him at some point, and that it should have been before they went to bed together. But it had happened so quickly. Hadn't they just been talking about his farm, when out of the blue, he'd kissed her? And now he's drinking beer at nine o'clock in the morning.

Does his behavior mean that he has secrets too? Or regrets?

'Look, I do not do that. Kiss and make love to strange women.'

'Me neither,' Frida shakes her head.

A smile spreads across Andrei's face.

'I'm glad.'

'I mean strange men,' Frida says and grins back at him.

'So, you haven't got a wife and ten kids back home?' Frida adds. She means it as a joke, but Andrei's face drops.

'Because in backward Romania we don't understand how, how do you say it, protection works?'

Frida is horrified. Had she made some crude generalization?

'No, that's not what...' but she doesn't have time to finish her sentence. Andrei leans closer, so that she can see the pupils of her dark eyes. And those lips.

'I'm sorry. I feel a bit, a bit out of place, here. That is all. I know you good woman. You have let me sleep in your home and you were good friend to my brother. I am sorry.'

He kisses Frida's mouth. The feel of his lips on her skin sends an electric charge through her body so strong that she has to pull away quickly. She stares at Andrei, who is startled by her action.

Frida doesn't want to ask why Andrei is so obviously upset this morning. But at the same time, she can't just jump into bed with him again. They need to talk.

Andrei looks puzzled for a moment and shrugs his shoulders. He takes a large gulp out of the bottle.

Frida gets up, goes over to the kitchen counter, and looks inside a brown china hen that Alicia gave her to store eggs in.

'So, omelet?' She asks, turning around to face Andrei again.

They make eye contact and Frida's heart leaps into her mouth. Andrei's eyes are even darker than they were before, and his gaze is so intense, Frida has to steady herself by taking hold of the counter behind her. All she wants to do is keep kissing those lips.

'Why you so kind to me?' Andrei asks.

Frida looks away for a moment. She walks slowly toward the table and stands in front of him.

Making eye contact with him, she says, 'Daniel was a good friend.'

Something in the tone of her voice betrays her and Andrei's eyebrows shoot up.

'Just a friend?'

Frida sighs.

She sits down next to him, and with her hands in her lap, not daring to look fully at Andrei's face, she whispers, 'Daniel is Anne Sofie's father.'

CHAPTER THIRTY-ONE

The labor issue on the farm is constantly on Alicia's mind.

She's sitting in her office, reviewing the farm accounts. It's the day when Leo, her real father, is arriving in Åland. It's the first time he will see Hilda again after their brief meeting some three months ago. Alicia is a little nervous about how the visit will go, although Hilda has assured her she is looking forward to meeting Leo again.

Alicia has finally made a decision, partly so that she can get the farm issue out of her mind and enjoy her time with Leo.

In the end, she just had to give into Lars. Her farm manager has now organized two Eastern European boys to come and work for the summer harvest. They should be arriving next week.

Hilda has agreed to let Alicia have one of her cottages to house them, as Uffe used to do. The conversation with her mom was easier than Alicia had expected.

Perhaps Hilda had been nervous about the prospect of having Leo under the same roof as her, and not thought the cottage issue through? Letting Alicia have the cottage means she will not get any rental income from it for the rest of the season.

Alicia had pointed this out to her mom, but she had assured her that it wasn't a problem.

Alicia knows that Hilda's new B&B venture hasn't been as successful as she had hoped, so perhaps she'd rather give it to Alicia than face the disappointment of not filling the cottage for the summer?

Whatever the reason, Lars had been delighted with Alicia's decision. But Alicia is still uneasy.

There is a hollow feeling in her gut, as if she is making a grave mistake.

This is probably the reason she hasn't told Patrick about her decision, although she did have a long conversation with Liam about it. She can see the irony in the way she can talk to her estranged husband about matters that are concerning her more easily than she can with Patrick.

She can't quite understand why, but when she speaks with Patrick, she is often filled with anger – no annoyance – rather than love or even fondness.

When she mentioned these feelings to Connie, her grief counsellor, she had asked Alicia is she felt abandoned by Patrick.

Alicia had taken a long time to reply.

'I guess I do.'

Alicia heard from Connie's voice that the woman was smiling at the other end of the telephone.

'When it was really you who decided to leave Stockholm, and with it, Patrick, wasn't it?'

Alicia has been thinking a lot about this, the last conversation with Connie. She did leave him, but somehow, she now realizes she had expected Patrick to come back to the islands with her.

She is also annoyed about the constant situation with Mia Eriksson. She is made to feel like the other woman by the whole family. Just the other day, she saw Beatrice, Mia's mom, in the supermarket. The woman turned her back on her as if she was a disreputable woman.

When Alicia and Patrick were newly in love, that kind of behavior would have made her laugh, but now, she's getting tired of it.

She is a full member of the island community, a farmer in her own right, so she should not be treated like some kind of marriage wrecker. Especially as it was Mia who wanted a divorce in the first place!

None of this, of course, is Patrick's fault, so why is Alicia taking it out on him?

Alicia puts her head in her hands and rubs her forehead with the heels of her palms.

Why does it have to be so complicated? Is the peripheral mess of their relationship making her love Patrick less?

CHAPTER THIRTY-TWO

Hilda sees a rental pull up the drive. She'd been debating with herself whether to go out and greet her ex-husband but then decided to let Alicia do it. She told her daughter that she would wait inside the house. Now, with the weather glorious, the sun shining in a blue, cloudless sky, staying indoors seems foolish, petty even.

Still, Hilda stands in the kitchen, watching as an older version of the first love of her life emerges from the car. She's surprised how well the man looks. He's lost weight, the paunch that he had when she saw him last has disappeared and his light brown hair has grown out and touches the collar of his polo shirt. He smiles widely at Alicia and the two hug warmly.

Tears prick Hilda's eyelids at the sight. Then, she's filled with anger. How can this man who so nearly ruined her life look so happy? He doesn't deserve Alicia's love, which Hilda now sees he has gained. She inhales deeply and tells herself to calm down. Hasn't she decided to forgive Leo? Hasn't she decided to be a grown-up about something that happened over forty years ago?

Hilda fixes a smile on her face and goes to open the door.

'Hello there,' she says, trying to sound friendly.

Suddenly she's regretting her promise of letting the man stay with her in the house. She has no other guests at the moment, so she thought it would be fine. But what had she been thinking?

When Leo steps up to the door and takes Hilda's hand in his, her heart flips. His fingers around hers seem so familiar, and warm. There is a twinkle in his eyes that she hadn't seen when they met in the Italian café last April. An age ago, it seems, because it was before Hilda lost Uffe.

They stand there, facing each other, while Alicia looks on.

'Can we come in, Mom?'

How long have they been standing there, gazing at each other's eyes? Hilda has gone into a trance, and only emerges from it when she hears her daughter's words.

She shakes her head, lets go of Leo's hand, and steps back from the doorway.

'Of course, please!'

'Would you like some coffee?' Hilda asks with her back to both Alicia and Leo.

'Yes please,' Leo replies.

Alicia has followed her mom to the other side of the kitchen.

'Mom, I've got to go, Lars wants to talk to me urgently.'

'Oh,' Hilda turns to face her daughter. At the same time, she sees that Leo is standing in the middle of the kitchen, rubbing his hands together. He looks awkward.

'Please, make yourself at home.'

Hilda stretches her hand out to indicate one of the kitchen chairs arranged around the table by a window overlooking the drive. She's set it up with three cups and a plateful of cinnamon buns.

Alicia lays a hand on Hilda's arm.

'Sorry.'

'I baked these earlier,' Hilda says to Leo as she pours coffee into their cups.

'They look tasty,' he says but doesn't take one.

Hilda seats herself down opposite the man and lifts up the plate of buns, offering it to him.

Leo brings his hand up, his open palm toward her.

'I'm sorry, I'm on a strict diet. Doctor's orders.'

Hilda nods. She feels a deep sense of rejection, which she knows is silly. She can't look at Leo, and there's a silence, until she thinks of something.

'You look well.'

Leo gives her a smile and his face takes on a boyish air. Hilda is transported back to Helsinki and the night they met at the gig. Leo and his band were playing. She was just a girl in the audience, and she'd been so delighted when Leo came over to talk to her.

She'd fallen in love with the lanky boy on the spot. Or had she just been a bit starstruck? No, she had truly loved Leo.

They got married quickly, just three months later, after finding out that Hilda was pregnant. Would they have got married if she'd had an abortion like her parents had wanted? But Hilda couldn't do that – she wanted the baby so much and believed in their love and future together. How foolish she'd been! Not that she regrets having Alicia. She's the best thing that ever happened to her. But Leo – she should never have trusted him.

'I've lost 15 kilos,' Leo now says proudly.

'It suits you.'

Hilda almost blushes when she realizes she's been thinking about their lovemaking. Leo was the most attentive of lovers. Hilda had only been with one boy before him, and it had been a fumble in the cramped back seat of a Lada. With Leo, it was natural and passionate. They could not take their hands off each other.

Until she had Alicia.

'I'll show you to your room,' Hilda says.

CHAPTER THIRTY-THREE

L eo is glad to be able to escape the oppressive, yet charged, atmosphere between him and his ex-wife. When he refused to eat the cinnamon buns Hilda had baked, it was as if he'd slapped her in the face. He'd not known that she'd become such a proud homemaker.

As he follows Hilda up the stairs, he gets a glimpse of a smartly furnished lounge. That and the recently fitted, immaculate kitchen with a fashionable island in the middle, are a far cry from their rented one-bedroom apartment in Kallio, then a working-class part of Helsinki.

Hilda stops at the first landing and, turning right, opens a door to a large bedroom. Leo walks in and takes in the view of a small cottage opposite the house, and beyond that the sea.

'This is nice,' Leo says and turns toward Hilda. Who is standing by the doorway.

She's wearing a pair of light blue slacks and a loose

blouse with tiny flowers on it. The color of the top matches that of her eyes. Leo has been trying not to look too deeply into those blue eyes, but now, seeing her standing, he sees there is a sadness to them.

'This used to be Stefan's room,' she says.

Leo looks around. He sees that motorbike wallpaper and a framed picture of a young boy, held tightly by Alicia, on the little chest of drawers. He goes toward the cabinet.

'May I?'

Hilda nods.

'A good-looking lad,' Leo says after studying the image for a moment.

Hilda comes to stand next to him and runs her fingers, painted a bright red color, down the glass of the picture. She sighs and turns to Leo.

'I'll leave you to get settled. You can have a shower, if you like, but Alicia was thinking of putting the sauna on later?'

'A sauna will be great.'

Leo coughs and glances at Hilda.

'This is very kind of you.'

She nods and gives him a quick smile.

'No problem,' she says.

But after she's disappeared down the stairs, Leo has the distinct feeling that Hilda would rather he was anywhere but under her roof.

Alone in the room, Leo unpacks his small suitcase and decides to give Hilda a little time to herself. She seemed discombobulated by his presence, which isn't a surprise really. Leo, too, has a bunch of emotions swirling around in his head that he can't quite sort out, so he lies down on the bed and takes out his newly acquired iPad.

He looks at what he could do while he's in Åland. He wants to spend as much time with Alicia as possible, but he understood from their brief conversation on the phone before he left for the ferry in Helsinki yesterday, that she has her hands full on the farm. Scanning the tourist information on the screen, his eyelids feel heavy, and he falls fast asleep.

Leo doesn't hear the knocking on the door, and he only comes to when he sees Hilda standing by his bed.

'Sorry to wake you, but Alicia is asking after you.'

Leo licks his lips and wipes his mouth with the back of his hand.

'What time is it?'

'Gone five,' Hilda says.

'Goodness!'

Leo rubs his eyes and lifts himself up.

'I'll let you get sorted. We thought sauna and then dinner?'

Hilda gives him a quick smile. Her face is soft, and she seems to have lost the look of bewilderment she had earlier.

Leo gets up quickly and grabs a plastic bag.

'I didn't know what to get you, so there's a bottle of perfume for you and some beer. It's alcohol-free, I'm afraid. I don't, not since, you know. Well, I've given up.'

He hands the bag to Hilda, who takes it and stares at Leo.

'The doc told me if I don't mend my ways, I'll be six feet under before the year is out.'

Hilda still doesn't say anything and suddenly Leo remembers. Her husband died just a few months ago.

He steps closer to her and takes her hands into his, 'I'm so sorry, that was very tactless of me.'

Hilda shakes her head and pulls herself away from Leo's grip.

She doesn't look at him, but says, 'If it's OK with you, Alicia and I will go into the sauna now. You can go after us.'

Hilda turns on her heels and disappears from the room.

Leo sighs and sits back down on the bed. How is it possible that he is constantly putting his foot in it with Hilda? Why isn't he able to talk to her normally?

CHAPTER THIRTY-FOUR

L ater, Leo sits in the sauna by the sea and tries to relax as the hot steam from the ladle of water he threw on the stones hits his shoulders and back. It's a good sauna with a wood-fired stove, and the view to the sea from the little window is amazing. The reeds sway in the light breeze and he can see a sailing boat glide effortlessly past.

He sighs and closes his eyes, leaning back against the wooden wall.

It was so close.

He knows he'd had the biggest test since he changed his lifestyle for the better. When he'd come down the stairs into the kitchen, he saw there was a plate of small appetizers made out of tiny pieces of rye bread topped with smoked salmon dill. But it wasn't the snacks, which looked delicious, but the bottle of beer Hilda had placed on the table next to the food. An opener, carved out of a reindeer antler, sat next to the bottle. Leo knew that the beer was some kind of local brew, and he could taste it on his lips just by looking at it.

Quickly, as if to make sure he didn't change his mind, Leo grabbed the opener and flipped off the top of the bottle. He brought it to his lips. But at the scent of the alcohol coming from the bubbly top of the beer, he stopped.

Alicia's face, when she had greeted him earlier, flashed in front of his eyes and he forced his arm to place the bottle back down on the table. He sat there, fighting the urge to take a sip, just one small mouthful, to sample what he knew must be a delicious brew. A tiny tipple couldn't hurt, could it? He put his head in his hands and sat there fighting his demons. After a while, he got up. Determinedly, he grabbed the bottle, went over to the sink and poured away the contents.

What a waste.

In the fridge, he found the alcohol-free beer he'd bought on the ferry. Hungrily, he opened a can and drank it all in one go.

When the two women returned from the sauna, both wearing their dressing gowns, with towels wrapped around their heads, Leo had calmed down. He'd helped himself to another of his beers and began reading on his iPad.

'Your turn!' Alicia said and smiled at Leo.

Hilda glanced at the now half-empty can in front of Leo but said nothing.

.   .   .

Alicia told him about a little path leading to a wooden jetty where he could take a dip in the sea, but Leo knew the Baltic would be cold even this late in the season, so decided to give it a miss. Alicia, it seems, was a keen swimmer.

Hilda had rolled her eyes at him when her daughter suggested a dip in the sea to Leo. The exchange of looks between him and Hilda had given him hope that she wasn't angry anymore. Although he had no idea what she would have been angry about.

Apart from the obvious.

He'd thought that after more than forty years, she would have forgiven him by now. Especially as she had – according to Alicia – insisted Leo should stay in her house while on the islands.

'The sauna is hot now, but just make sure the fire doesn't go out. Throw a few logs into the stove if it needs it. They're stacked under the bench on the porch,' Hilda told him before he left the house.

She'd fussed about a towel and told him there was soap and shampoo in the little washroom next to the sauna. Leo was amazed about the change of mood, but he didn't say anything, just thanked Hilda and Alicia and left them.

As he made his way down to the shore, where the roof of the red sauna cottage was visible through a line of trees, he wondered what Hilda's husband, the late Uffe was like.

He must have been a good man, taking on another man's child. Alicia has told him that he was like a father to her, a comment that Leo has to admit had stung him at the time. But, of course, he hadn't been around, so why wouldn't she consider the man who brought her up as her dad?

Making amends seems like an insurmountable task. Sometimes Leo wonders why he's trying so hard, but then he remembers how he felt when he returned to Helsinki after meeting Alicia and Hilda again last spring. How he'd been hungover and feeling sorry for himself. How he'd felt so very lonely, and how regrets about the past and opportunities missed haunted him. Predictably, he'd gone on another bender, drinking himself silly again.

It was a phone call from Alicia one evening about two weeks after they'd met on the islands, that changed everything. She'd asked him how he was, and he'd slurred out something.

'Drunk?' She had simply asked, and Leo had felt such shame that he'd been unable to reply.

'Well, suit yourself,' she'd added and put down the phone.

Leo had listened to the empty tone of his cell for several minutes. He'd gone to his sink and drunk a large glass of water. He'd taken the bottle of Koskenkorva he was drinking and emptied it down the sink, doing the same with cans of beer he had in the fridge.

The next morning was terrible. After a restless night when he'd dreamed of Alicia, Hilda, and the grandson he'd never met, hovering above him, pointing their fingers and accusing him of killing the boy, he phoned the health center. He made an appointment with his doctor, who prescribed some medication and enrolled him on a program for alcoholics.

'But I'm not an alcoholic,' Leo had protested.

The doctor, a young woman with cropped hair and a thin build, had lifted her eyebrows.

'Why are you here then?'

Leo had stared at her. There was a silence that lasted several minutes.

'See how you get on,' the young doctor had said, giving him the prescription and a leaflet about the program.

'You're in luck. There's a space on the next lot of sessions, which start today. This is the address. I think it's in Kaisaniemi.' She pointed at the piece of paper in Leo's hand. 'Be there at 3pm.'

He'd now been sober for four months and five days. It was still difficult, but he was determined. And he felt so much better. The healthy diet he was on helped, as did the yoga classes he'd started taking.

He smiles when he thinks back to when he told his drinking pal, Simo, about his life changes.

'Yoga? You?' Simo had said and taken a long swig out of his glass of beer. Leo had been drinking his zero alcohol Koff.

That was the last time he'd seen Simo. It just wasn't the same watching his friend, and everyone else in the pub, getting drunk. They all looked so silly, and sense-less, repeating themselves all the time, and getting louder the more they drank.

Leo was embarrassed for his friend and wondered if he had behaved so stupidly when they went out drinking together. He was certain he had. Simo had noticed something wasn't right with Leo and had got aggressive, accusing him of judging his friend. Leo realized that there was no friendship with Simo without alcohol.

At home that same evening, Leo was sad he'd lost a buddy, but proud that he hadn't been tempted to join Simo drinking. It had been hard at first, but as the evening drew on, Leo had been more and more pleased that he was sober.

But now Hilda's attitude toward him, which seems to turn hot and cold at the snap of her fingers, has made him crave a drink more than anything in the past months.

CHAPTER THIRTY-FIVE

W hen Leo steps inside the kitchen, more relaxed after the sauna, he notices that mother and daughter have changed into summer dresses.

'There you are!' Hilda says, turning around from the sink, where the two women have been preparing a salad.

'We thought we'd eat outside on the deck? It's such a lovely evening.'

Alicia comes over and gives Leo a quick hug.

'That will be great,' Leo replies and adds, 'Do I have time to get changed quickly?'

'Of course,' Hilda says, turning back to the sink.

A few moments later Alicia and Leo are sitting at a teak table, covered with a pale cloth dotted with pink flowers.

'Everything OK?' Alicia asks. Her face is full of concern.

'Yes, why?'

'I just thought...'

'What?' Leo examines Alicia's expression.

'Mom said you'd had one of the local beers that she'd left for you.'

Leo shakes his head.

'No, I didn't. I opened it before realizing. I poured it down the sink. I'm sorry.'

Leo takes Alicia's hand into his. 'I promised you.'

Alicia's face lights up.

'I'm so relieved! I didn't tell Mom about you being sober until just now. I don't know why, I just thought it was up to you to tell her if you wanted to.'

'It's OK.'

'No, it isn't. I should have told her before.'

At that point, Hilda comes out, carrying a large tray. As she places it on the table, Leo sees to his horror that it bears a huge side of sliced beef. Pink in the middle, it has been marinated in something and appears to be cold, surrounded by a colorful salad.

'Please, help yourself,' Hilda says, proudly looking at the food.

Leo is quiet for a moment, glancing from Alicia to Hilda.

'Go on, you must be starving after the nap and sauna,' Hilda says.

'I'm so sorry, I didn't tell you ...' Leo says.

Hilda looks up at him, her eyes sharp.

'What now? You don't eat food either?'

Leo is so taken aback that he doesn't know what to say next.

'Don't worry, there's no alcohol on the beef or the

salad. Or the new potatoes, for that matter. Just a knob of butter on the top.'

Hilda lifts the lid on a china dish next to Leo.

'Mom!' Alicia says.

Nobody speaks for a moment.

'Well, if my food isn't good enough for you lot, I'm going to help myself.'

Hilda piles her plate up with several pieces of meat, a bunch of salad and potatoes.

Alicia sighs and also serves herself with everything.

'Go on, Leo,' she says, passing a set of long salad tongs to him.

Leo takes them but immediately puts them down on the plate.

'I'm so sorry, Hilda, but I'm vegan.'

'What?'

CHAPTER THIRTY-SIX

'First you accuse me of tempting him with alcohol, when I didn't know he was on the wagon, and then you forget to tell me he's on some kind of new-fangled, new-age diet!'

Alicia and Hilda are in the kitchen where Hilda is shouting at her daughter.

Alicia sighs. She has enough on her mind without her parents rowing. She cannot make sense of what Daniel's brother is inferring about the Romanian boy's death. Or if Dudnikov was involved in it all. Not to mention that she's just agreed to employ East European labor on the farm again.

She urgently needs to talk to Lars, and to Ebba, but she hasn't decided what she should say or do.

What if Uffe was involved? Alicia gazes at her mom. Instead, she's here babysitting her estranged parents who are both of an age to know better than to bicker all the time.

'He was OK. He had some salad and potatoes,' she says, and hears how feeble she sounds.

'Just as well I'd left some without butter on them in the pan!' Hilda replies.

'Which means he isn't starving.'

When her mom doesn't reply, or even look at Alicia, she continues, 'Isn't it enough punishment that he didn't see his only daughter grow up? And that he never met his one and only grandchild?'

This time Alicia is more adamant. To soften the blow of her words, she goes to hug her mom. Hilda's body feels rigid at first, but then she relaxes into her daughter's embrace.

'You'll see, it'll be fine. Leo is like a different person, and it's so great to see. He's given up alcohol and meat for a healthier lifestyle. Isn't that admirable?'

'I guess,' Hilda mutters and places a plate in the dishwasher.

'I'm sorry to have caused you so much trouble,' Leo says.

Neither woman has heard him come down the stairs. Leo had excused himself after dinner and Alicia thought he'd gone to bed. But here he stood, in his deep blue dressing gown, probably alarmed by their angry voices. His feet are bare, and Alicia can see a deep scar along one of his legs, which makes him look vulnerable.

Doesn't her mother know that he has been seriously ill?

Hilda turns to face Leo. With her arms crossed over her chest, she says, 'It's only polite to let your host know if you're on some kind of peculiar diet.'

There's real hostility in her voice.

Alicia tries to think of something to say to defuse the situation, but all she wants to do is flee to her own cottage across the yard. She knows it's her fault Leo is here, so she stays, even though it's highly painful to see her parents row like this.

When Hilda and Uffe had disagreements, she used to find it funny more than worrying. They never really fought – it was more a case of her mother nagging her stepfather. Alicia would often take his side, especially when she was a teenager, which she knew annoyed Hilda, but for some reason none of their bickering ever seemed serious. Now Hilda appears to be angry about more than just Leo's veganism or refusal to drink alcohol.

'You're right and I'm sorry,' Leo says and adds, 'But I really didn't expect you to cook me dinner.'

'Well, that's just ridiculous!' Hilda barks.

Alicia can see her mother is even more riled by Leo's comment.

Leo sighs and stretches his arms out, opening up his palms.

'I very much enjoyed the salad and potatoes. And the sauna was lovely. It's very kind of you to put me up like this, but it's probably best if I move to one of the hotels in Mariehamn.'

'You'd like that, wouldn't you? Show me up to everyone! How I can't look after my guests, so they have to find other accommodation.'

Hilda's voice is dangerously low. It's as if she's hissing at Alicia's father.

Alicia takes hold of her mother's arm and looks at Leo. 'No one is going anywhere tonight. Let's all calm down and talk about it in the morning?'

Leo and Hilda stare at each other.

'Mom?' Alicia asks, moving her eyes away from Leo.

'I don't want anyone to leave! All I want is a little consideration, that's all,' Hilda shrieks.

Leo takes a few steps into the kitchen from the doorway where he'd stopped a few minutes earlier. He speaks softly, addressing Hilda.

'Look, I don't want to leave either. Your house is wonderful. I am so sorry I didn't let you know that there are things I cannot eat – or drink – now. I will try to be more considerate in the future.'

Leo takes another step closer, so that he's facing Hilda.

'If you let me stay, that is,' he adds.

Hilda straightens her back and says, 'Of course you can stay.'

She turns away from Leo and Alicia and closes the dishwasher door with a loud bang.

'I think it's time we all turned in, don't you?' she says, turning back to face Leo and Alicia, who are standing still, watching her every move, as if she could involuntarily combust.

'Good idea,' Leo says. He nods toward Hilda and Alicia and leaves the kitchen.

'Are you OK?' Alicia asks her mother, who's watching the door through which Leo has just vanished.

Hilda is startled.

'I was miles away,' she says and hugs Alicia. 'Off you

go too. You've got an early start, haven't you? I'll finish up here,' she says, dismissing her daughter.

Alicia wishes her mom goodnight and thanks her for dinner. As she turns to leave, she adds, 'If it's too much to have him here, I could find him somewhere else. No one would know he came from us, honestly.'

'No, he's staying here. That's my final word.' Hilda says without turning to look at Alicia.

Breakfast is equally awkward. Leo and Hilda are hardly speaking to each other.

'I thought I might go shopping for some vegan items, so that you wouldn't have to worry,' Leo says after he's finished eating, but his comment is met with a snort from Alicia's mom.

They're sitting outside on the deck again. The sun is so bright that Hilda has put up the two large parasols. Alicia has noticed that Leo has only eaten a piece of rye bread with a few slices of tomato and cucumber.

As well as the vegetables, Hilda had also set out three kinds of bread, ham, slices of Edam cheese, a bowl of berries, and three pots of yogurt. Earlier, when she saw the breakfast table, Alicia wondered why her mother was serving so many things Leo can't eat. Is this some kind of protest?

'That's a great idea, we could go into town together. I need to see someone there anyway,' Alicia says to Leo.

She glances at her mom, who immediately says, 'Why don't you cook your own meals too, so that I don't poison you by mistake.'

Hilda gets up and takes everyone's plates inside.

Alicia rolls her eyes and rises from the table. As she stretches across to take the plate with the ham and cheese, Leo grabs her wrist and gets up too.

'Let me.'

His face is determined, but Alicia isn't sure it's a good idea for him to go after her mom now.

'Are you sure? She can be quite temperamental.'

Leo smiles at Alicia.

'Don't worry, I know your mother.'

CHAPTER THIRTY-SEVEN

'Hello Brit, how are you? Are you feeling OK?'

Alicia is glad to hear from her oldest friend, who returned to the islands from her glamorous life on Caribbean cruise liners about the same time Alicia did. She is now five months pregnant with her first child, and Alicia cannot help worrying about her. She's approaching forty, like herself, so there could be complications. Alicia has agreed that if Jukka, her sea captain boyfriend, is away and cannot get back in time, she will be her birthing partner.

'I'm fine Alicia! In the blooming stage.'

'Huh, good to hear,' Alicia laughs, then adds, 'I know that, of course, but I worry.'

'Yeah, but there's no need. And Jukka is home tomorrow morning.'

'That's good.'

'Look, could we meet up? I'm going crazy here at home on my own.'

'Is everything OK?'

In the past, a call like this from Brit would have been highly normal. They often met up in town for a drink at short notice when Brit was ashore. Brit also used to work on the cruise ships between Finland and Sweden but gave up her job as a restaurant manager when she fell pregnant. Alicia hopes her friend isn't regretting this decision, which she knows was made largely at Jukka's behest. He's quite old-fashioned when it comes to women and pregnancies.

'Yes, everything is fine. Will you come here?'

'Now?'

'If you can?'

'Of course!'

Alicia can hear her friend exhale loudly.

What is going on?

'Great, there's a glass of wine for you in it.'

'In that case!'

Now Alicia smiles. Perhaps her friend is just bored after all?

'See you later,' Brit says and disconnects the call.

Alicia is glad to escape the frosty atmosphere between her mom and Leo.

She left them in the kitchen after another awkward meal. Alicia and Leo had been to town that morning to buy some vegan supplies, but Hilda hadn't been pacified by the fact that she didn't need to cook for him anymore. Rather, she seemed hurt that she was being bypassed in the kitchen.

Leo just can't win.

As she drives past the slowly darkening canal and over the low swing bridge, Alicia realizes it was a bad idea to bring him to the islands. Or at least, she should have insisted that he stay in town. She sees the lights of the Arkipelag hotel reflected on the water of the East Harbor in the distance and thinks how much easier it would have been if he'd stayed there. She could have arranged a meal for the three of them, and they could have come together on neutral ground. But she had no idea how prickly Hilda would be with her real father. Thank goodness, he is returning to Helsinki the day after tomorrow.

When she takes a left, which leads up to the hill where the new Solberget residential area is, Alicia's thoughts turn toward her friend.

Who would have imagined that Brit, the girl who never wanted to settle down, least of all back on the islands, would now be pregnant with a local sea captain's baby?

She wonders why Brit wanted her to come over so suddenly, and frowns. Did she have concerns over the baby?

Alicia herself has only given birth once, and that was nearly twenty years ago now. But you never forget what it's all about. She's certain, if it came to it, she'd be able to calm Brit down and help her with the birth. Thinking and talking about the baby is far easier than her present worries with the farm and her bickering parents!

. . .

'What?'

Alicia is stunned by what Brit has told her.

'Look, my dad meets up with his old friends, you know the same group that Uffe used to see for a beer?'

Brit gives Alicia a careful look.

'And they said what exactly?'

'According to them, Patrick phoned two of the farmers and asked whether they employed East European labor and if so, could he interview them.'

'And what did they say?'

Brit smiles.

'What do you think? They refused, of course. Patrick isn't exactly popular here on the islands, what with leaving Eriksson's beloved daughter and ...'

Alicia puts her hand up.

'The fact is that Mia had an affair and left him, but that's not something the Erikssons advertise!'

'I know, I know!' Brit exclaims and Alicia apologizes.

She is just so frustrated with the whole situation with Patrick and his ex. But, more to the point, what an earth is he playing at contacting Uffe's old friends? She told him about the labor issue in confidence, not so that he could go discussing it with all and sundry.

'Anyway, I thought you should know. I'm not sure what this is all about, but it just seemed a bit odd to Dad. And it does seem strange to me too.'

'Isn't it!' Alicia says. She's rubbing her fingers against her bottom lip.

'Do you know what he's doing?'

Brit's eyebrows are raised, and her face is a veritable question mark.

Alicia shrugs her shoulders.

'I really don't know. But thank you for telling me.'

'Are you sure? I don't want to interfere, but ...'

Her friend is gazing at Alicia. Her face feels hot under Brit's scrutiny.

'It's OK. I'll talk to him.'

'Oh, and I nearly forgot, did you know that Frida has a new boyfriend?'

Alicia laughs. Nothing is secret for long on these islands.

'Yes and no. You probably mean Andrei. He's Daniel's brother. You know the poor boy who drowned? I don't think they are an item. How did you know about him?' she asks.

'Not from you!' Brit says and gives Alicia a playfully reproachful look.

'Sorry, with my mom and Leo and the farm, I just haven't had a moment to myself.'

Brit puts her hand over Alicia's.

They're sitting on a sofa facing the wonderful view of the Slemmern water and the lights of Mariehamn beyond it.

'Don't worry, I'm just teasing. I have nothing better to do but to gossip with the other island folk.' Brit grins at Alicia. 'I hear he's very good-looking,' she adds.

'Yes, and very nice,' Alicia replies, and continues, 'but how on earth do you know about him?

'One of the mothers in my birthing class has a child

at the same nursery as Anne Sofie. The Romanian came with Frida to collect the baby the other day.'

'Of course,' Alicia laughs. 'I keep forgetting what a small place this is.'

'And you've met him?'

Alicia regards her friend for a moment.

'Yes. The thing is, you remember Anne Sofie is really Daniel's daughter?'

Brit nods, then her mouth opens. She places a hand over it.

'Ah, now I get it. Does the guy know this?

'Don't think so, and I have a feeling Frida wants to keep it that way, so if you wouldn't mind, please don't tell anyone?'

Brit moves her thumb and forefinger across her mouth in a gesture of zipping up her lips.

'Scout's honor.'

'Thank you. It's a bit of a tricky situation. He's asking a lot of questions about the poor boy's death.'

'I guess that's natural?' Brit says and yawns.

Alicia looks at her friend.

'You look tired. Let's call it a night?'

Brit nods.

'You don't mind me telling you about Patrick, do you?'

'No, it's probably just a misunderstanding.'

Brit doesn't reply. She gazes at Alicia, as if waiting for more details, but Alicia manages to convince her friend to make it an early night.

She does feel guilty for keeping her thoughts about

the farm from Brit, but she can't tell another person about her labor issue with Lars.

She trusts her friend, but it's already enough that Patrick is stirring things up. What if Brit said something to her father, say, and Alicia's dilemma is discussed by Uffe's old friends. Not only would she be a laughing stock, but it would completely undermine her authority with Lars too. The talk would no doubt reach his ears sooner or later.

Alicia just hopes that Patrick's actions haven't already damaged her relationship with the farm manager.

It's just coming up to nine o'clock, and the buildings in Mariehamn, on the opposite shore of Slemmern, shine brightly on the water. Grädhyllan – Cream Shelf as the locals call the area – is a beautiful place to live, Alicia thinks, as she opens her car and steps inside.

As she drives back down the hill, and turns left toward Sjoland, Alicia has a sudden thought. What would Patrick say if she decided to sell the farm after all? They could buy an apartment close to where Brit and Jukka live, and Patrick could work at the local paper again. Would he do that for her? Alicia isn't so sure.

CHAPTER THIRTY-EIGHT

W hen Leo enters the kitchen, Hilda has her back to him. Her shoulders are hunched, and her head bent forward, but she doesn't seem to be doing anything, just standing there.

'Hilda,' Leo starts.

His ex-wife turns quickly on her heels and he sees that her eyes are filled with tears.

'I'm so sorry,' Leo says and walks up to her, placing the plate on top of the kitchen countertop.

'It's not your fault,' Hilda sniffs and wipes her eyes carefully, so as not to disturb her makeup.

Without thinking what he is doing, Leo puts his arms around Hilda. She feels small inside his embrace, but instead of softening her muscles, Leo feels them tense.

'Get off me!'

Leo takes a step back, letting his arms drop by his sides. Hilda's face is full of fury.

'How dare you!'

'I didn't ...'

But Leo doesn't have a chance to explain.

'I have just lost my husband. I took you in out of the goodness of my heart, and this is how you reward me? Trying to take advantage of me? I should have known. You'll never change!'

Hilda walks swiftly past Leo and dashes up the stairs.

Leo is stunned.

How could he have read the situation so wrongly? How could Hilda have misunderstood his intentions so fundamentally? All he thought he was doing was comforting his ex-wife. It's not as if he's some kind of stranger. They were married once! Admittedly a long time ago but all the same.

Leo sinks onto a kitchen chair and rubs his chin.

I need to go back to Helsinki. This is too difficult.

Why couldn't Hilda see that he had stopped drinking because of her? And Alicia.

During his sessions with the AA, he had come to realize that his drinking was an attempt to escape the memory of that time when – out of his skull on alcohol – he had slapped Hilda. It was something he was going to regret as long as he lived. But, and this is the real reason he is here, he needs to seek forgiveness from Hilda.

He has already talked to Alicia about it all, and she told him she understood and forgave him. That was such a relief to Leo, and he had hugged and kissed his daughter. Alicia had just laughed, but from the tears pooling in her eyes, he understood that the moment had meant a lot to her too.

Hilda is turning out to be far more complicated.

He had expected the visit to be difficult, but he hadn't been prepared for the hostility to be directed at his sobriety and veganism.

A thought occurs to Leo.

Perhaps Hilda is using his new healthy lifestyle as an excuse to be angry at him? Is it possible that she is still mad at him, but can't admit that it's because of what happened forty years ago?

With this new insight, Leo feels more confident. He will try to talk to Hilda, try to explain how awful he has felt since that terrible night. He will make every effort to explain that all the changes he has made to his life are because of Hilda and Alicia. Perhaps this way, he might get through to her?

CHAPTER THIRTY-NINE

Patrick reads what he has written four times before pressing send. It's a whole week since his editor issued an ultimatum of sorts, and since then, each time Patrick has seen the old man, he has given Patrick a long stare. There have been several emails asking for his story, by Jan Axelsson himself, as well as the features editor, a frighteningly efficient woman called Lina Snell. He was even asked to attend the production meeting earlier in the week, chaired by Lina. At the meeting, Axelsson had made him promise the full text of an article by close of play on Friday.

It's just gone midnight and Patrick can hear the young revellers on the street below. He wants to go out and have a beer himself, that's what he usually does after finishing an assignment, but tonight is different.

He has no desire to celebrate.

He knows the article is a good one – Axelsson has seen the first draft and told Patrick that it would be one of the features in the Sunday edition. It's the first time

Patrick has made the weekend paper since he came back to *Journalen,* so he should be over the moon with his work.

But ...

He knows he shouldn't have written the story.

Not this one.

He's tried to keep Alicia's late stepfather's name out of it, but he's not sure he's done enough. He stares at the screen and checks that the email has gone, and that the article is also posted onto the paper's portal. No one has yet seen it, so he could still pull it if he wanted to.

Patrick gets up from his desk and finds a bottle of whisky that he bought from the ferry the last time he went to see Alicia on the islands. It's a rather special Lagavulin 16-year-old single malt, which he had decided to save for special occasions. As he pours a two-finger width into the glass, he tries not to think about Alicia.

Yet, sipping his drink by the open window, staring blankly at the rooftops of the turn-of-the-century apartment blocks in his beloved Söder, he can't keep his thoughts away from Alicia. He remembers the way she sighs when they make love, her endearing habit of pushing a strand of hair behind her ear when she is flustered or can't think of a reply to a difficult question. Her smile is etched onto his brain. Oh, how he misses her scent, the feel of her body beneath his own.

He knows he doesn't deserve her love – only a few months ago he betrayed her with his ex-wife. Mia was lonely when, predictably, the man she had left him for dumped her. She wanted to get back together, 'for the sake of our daughters' as she put it.

But soon, it was clear to Patrick that Mia wouldn't stay faithful to him. And he'd never been good enough for the wealthy Eriksson family. His parents were normal working people, and he was raised in northern Sweden, with a hint of a Dalarna accent, which in Stockholm stood out.

Over the years, Patrick had worked hard on losing his accent, which funnily enough, was close to the Åland intonation. It was partly why he had felt at home on the islands and with Mia.

It was only later that he realized the extent of the Eriksson family's snobbery. Their desire to keep up appearances was so deep that Kurt had even tried to advance Patrick's career by asking his editor to promote him.

Axelsson and Kurt knew each other, but to the editor's credit, he had refused to be swayed. Patrick got no favors from the old man and had worked his way up in the traditional manner, with hard work.

The divorce was an embarrassing stain on the Eriksson clan's reputation on the islands, but Patrick thinks getting rid of an unsuitable son-in-law was more important.

Patrick was grateful to Axelsson for taking him back after his resignation the previous summer. He'd been going through the divorce from Mia, which was acrimonious to say the least, and at the same time he'd met and fallen for Alicia.

What a summer that was!

All he'd wanted then was to stay on the islands, to be near Alicia and his own daughters.

His face goes into a smirk when he thinks about what Kurt Eriksson will make of his story. Again, he didn't mention his former in-laws, but surely, they must have been aware of what was going on? Kurt had his fingers in many pies both on the islands and across the water in Stockholm.

Patrick thinks back to his research and what a stroke of luck – or not – it was to find the name of the company used by the farm managers to syphon off funds. Registered in the Cayman Islands, the company have many dealings in Stockholm too, but the surprising element was the connection to Åland.

That was the sensational element of the story and the one that interested Axelsson. 'Who would have thought that the idyllic island community is holding such a dirty secret? That there is a criminal underbelly even there? That in itself is a scoop. Can't you see it? And with your local knowledge, you are the perfect person to write the story.'

The balding editor had been staring at Patrick during the features meeting, when he'd tried to play down the significance of the story. The money involved was just a tenth of that being made in similar operations suspected in Sweden, Patrick had argued, and he'd proposed digging deeper into local criminality, rather than concentrating on the island connection.

What will Alicia say when she inevitably reads the article? Or when the local newspapers and social media get hold of it. Should he warn her? But what will he tell her? That her beloved Uffe might have been involved in people trafficking?

CHAPTER FORTY

It's Sunday morning and the first thought Alicia has is that Leo is going back to Helsinki today. The relief is palpable. She's been watching the atmosphere between her mom and her real father become more and more tense, so much so that last night they hardly said a word to each other.

Alicia had left them to it again, saying she was tired and retiring to her cottage across the yard as soon as she'd finished her meal.

It'd only been nine o'clock and Hilda's eyes had shot up when Alicia made her announcement. But she couldn't do anything for them – they would always hate each other, and she had tried to bring them together. Why couldn't they at least try to be friends?

She'd convinced herself that her presence might even make matters worse, as they each seem to try to get her on their side. Still, she felt bad fleeing like that. Battling with guilt, she'd quickly hugged each of them goodnight, before she could change her mind, and left them to it.

As Alicia comes to, she realizes there's a ping from her cell, then another, and another.

She picks up the device and sees that she has several WhatsApp messages. One is from Brit, one from Ebba, the Police Chief, and one from her old boss at the local newspaper, Harri Nousiainen.

She opens up Brit's messages first, fearing she's slept through a call to the hospital.

Alicia, you must read this.

There's a link to an article in *Journalen*, Patrick's paper.

Confused, Alicia doesn't open the article, but goes on to the message from the editor at *Ålandsbladet*. When she sees that there is a link to the same article in his message, another alert fills her screen. It's a text from Kurt Eriksson.

How did Kurt get her cell number?

Get in touch with me immediately. Do not, I repeat, DO NOT speak to any reporters, including Patrick. Regards, Kurt.

What is going on?

With shaking hands, she taps the link to the article and begins reading.

CHAPTER FORTY-ONE

Hilda finds Alicia slumped in her bed. It's past 10am and Leo has been trying to call her. He's been jittery about missing his ferry all morning even though it doesn't depart until after 2pm.

In the end, after Leo had tried calling Alicia, even Hilda became worried and decided to see why her daughter wasn't at breakfast as agreed. She'd left the table in such a hurry last night, Hilda had worried she was ill.

'Are you OK?'

Alicia nods, but doesn't look at Hilda. Her eyes are focused on the distance. Her shoulder-length hair is dishevelled, and she's still in her nightie. Her face is pale.

Hilda places a hand on her forehead, but Alicia isn't running a temperature.

'Is it your tummy?' Hilda says and sits down beside her. 'Give me your hand, I'll take your pulse.'

Alicia turns her head toward Hilda and pulls herself away.

'I'm perfectly fine.'

Her pale gray eyes are dark, and her voice as well as her expression are hostile.

Hilda doesn't understand. Is she still angry at her over Leo?

Alicia must realize she can't hide her anger and resentment, built up over decades, toward a man who more or less abandoned her with a young baby. Although it was her who left him, she corrects herself. But only after he'd struck her, for goodness sake!

'Leo and I had a chat last night, so it was right of you to leave us when you did. We are fine now. You mustn't worry about us.'

'As if I care!'

Alicia's voice is strangled, as if she is fighting tears. It reminds Hilda of when Alicia was in her teens and had discovered some perceived injustice.

But she is no longer a petulant teenager, she's practically a middle-aged woman. No, this must be something serious. Hilda scans her brain as she searches Alicia's face.

Her daughter gets up and makes her way to the little kitchen, between the farm office and her living quarters.

Hilda sighs and gets up too.

'What is the matter?'

Hilda is speaking to Alicia's back.

Her daughter tightens the cord around her baby-blue dressing gown. She takes coffee out of a cupboard, puts some into a cafetière and pops the kettle on.

Alicia turns around abruptly.

'You tell me! You say you don't have any idea how Uffe ran the farm. But you must have known how he organized the Eastern European boys? How they were brought here as modern-day slaves?'

Hilda can't speak. Her throat is dry, and she is scanning her memory for what Uffe told her about the Russian. How he had helped Lars with getting some labor for the farm. Involuntarily, she places her hand over her mouth.

Alicia takes a deep breath and pours hot water over the ground coffee.

'So, you knew,' she says almost in a whisper.

'No, no! I cannot believe Uffe would have...' Hilda starts, but Alicia stops her.

She pours herself a coffee. Not offering Hilda a drink, she turns on her heels and opens the door to the office.

'Read for yourself.'

Alicia points to her computer screen, which is filled with the text of a newspaper article. The headline reads:

Not so idyllic after all. Slave labor routinely brought to the Åland Islands.

'Sit,' Alicia says, indicating a chair. She gives Hilda an angry stare and disappears out of the room.

CHAPTER FORTY-TWO

Hilda cannot believe her eyes.

The article charts a practice, going on for 'at least ten years', whereby farmers on the islands get in cheap labor through a company registered on the Cayman Islands. It tells the story of a young man from Romania whose identity has not been revealed to save his family from any reprisals. How he is duped into traveling to the Åland islands. How his passport and any identification documents are confiscated during the long journey by bus. And how he is then paid a pittance for the hard work he does on the farm during the summer. The boys are given food and basic facilities in cramped accommodations, but work seven days a week for a fraction of the minimum wage. Yet most are still able to send money home.

The boy, only sixteen when he made the journey from home to a strange country, is told that once he has paid back the cost of the travel, he can have his passport back and can start the life in a rich country that he's always dreamed about.

When Hilda finishes the article, she scrolls to the top of the page. With horror, she sees the name at the top of the article.

'How...?' She says out loud.

'My guess is as good as yours!'

Hilda hasn't heard her daughter enter the office.

She turns around and sees that Alicia has put on a pair of jeans and a crumpled T-shirt. She sits on one of Uffe's old comfy chairs that she had refused to replace when they remodelled the cottage.

'Now's the time to tell me what you've been keeping secret all this time. I've asked Lars to come over too. I want to know what has been happening on this farm.'

Alicia's face is contorted, and her mouth is in a straight line. Hilda has never seen her daughter so angry. Or, rather, with such fury directed at her own mom.

'Darling, I've told you over and over that I don't know how Uffe ran his farm. I am certain none of this happened here!'

But even as Hilda utters the words, she recalls how Uffe said the Russian had helped him and Lars find cheap labor. But surely he couldn't have ...

Alicia must have read her thoughts, because she comes over and stands by the laptop. She has her hands crossed over her chest.

'I swear Mom, if you don't speak now, I will burst!'

'OK, there was that Russian, you know the one who threatened me in the shop.'

Hilda glances at her daughter, who hasn't moved.

'Go on,' she says through gritted teeth.

'It was Uffe who introduced me to him. He said ...'

Hilda can't go on. She is absolutely certain that her wonderful loving, straight-laced husband would not have agreed to such an arrangement. She can feel tears well behind her eyelids. She takes a deep intake of breath and carries on.

'He only said that the Russian helped him and Lars find labor. But Uffe would never have agreed to anything untoward. I am absolutely certain of that!'

Hilda looks at her daughter, and suddenly anger and irritation toward Alicia surges through her.

'How can *you* believe that your father would have done this?'

For a moment, Alicia looks abashed, but she quickly straightens herself.

'Because that's the evidence!'

She points at the computer screen.

'And who has written this article?'

Hilda is trying hard not to shout at Alicia. She is now so full of fury and indignation that she gets up and storms out of the farm office.

On second thoughts, she turns back at the front door and steps inside the office once more. Alicia is now sitting in front of the laptop, staring at the screen. When she hears Hilda beside her, she turns toward her mom. Her eyes are full of tears, and just like that, Hilda's heart melts.

She kneels down beside Alicia, puts her arms around her daughter and hugs her hard.

'Darling, we must not fall out. I am sure this will sort

itself out. You know as well as I do that Uffe could not have done this! He was the gentlest, fairest, most loving man I have ever known. I am certain what he agreed to was all above board and legal.'

Alicia sighs and leans into Hilda's embrace.

'I wish you were right.'

Suddenly Hilda realizes she's in a very uncomfortable position and fears her knees will give out at any moment.

'Ouch.'

Immediately, Alicia rises from her chair, takes hold of Hilda's arms, and helps her up.

'Are you OK?'

'Yes, just old age, dear.'

The two women stand for a moment in silence, both deep in their thoughts. Hilda wants to ask about Patrick, but she fears Alicia' reaction.

What a betrayal.

'I presume you didn't know about this?' Hilda says, carefully regarding her daughter's face.

Alicia just shakes her head. Again, she slumps down on the green velveteen chair in the corner.

With her hands covering her face, she says, 'I did talk to him about my suspicions.'

She gazes up at Hilda.

'You know I tried to talk to you too, but you didn't say anything about Dudnikov!'

Hilda sees the anger briefly resurfacing, but she hopes her daughter's rage is now directed where it should have been from the start: Patrick.

Hilda doesn't understand why he has done this. She

knows he's an ambitious man, and no doubt this scoop will be more than a feather in his cap, but she also believed that he truly loved Alicia.

'He must have realized how this would affect us, the farm – and you!'

Hilda's voice has risen and the words come out more forcefully than she intended.

Alicia nods.

'The worst of it is that I talked to him about my suspicions – or rather puzzlement - about the labor situation here.'

Alicia's eyes are filled with tears,

'Oh, Mom. I asked him to investigate!'

At that moment there's knock on the front door to the cottage.

'Hello, are you there?'

It's Leo.

Alicia's heart sinks even further. The last thing she needs is for her fighting parents to create another scene.

She needs time to think.

She needs to talk to Lars.

Surely the farm manager must know something about this! He knows everything that goes on in this place, so if the farm and Uffe have somehow been involved in this, he is the man who will know the truth.

Alicia gazes down at her cell but Lars hasn't replied to her messages. She tries his number again, just as Leo comes inside the office. Alicia turns her back on Hilda and Leo.

While she listens to the beeps at the other end, she hears Hilda take Leo out of the office and into the lounge. This is the fourth call Alicia has put through to the farm manager this morning, but once again, the call isn't answered. There's not even his usual greeting to leave a message.

Why isn't he answering?

CHAPTER FORTY-THREE

O n the day that Leo is due to return to Helsinki, things with Hilda have finally improved a little. As he sits in the sun-filled kitchen, nursing a cup of coffee, he thinks that in spite of the awkward moments, it has been wonderful to spend time with Alicia and Hilda. A year ago, he didn't imagine he would ever be here, with his only family. Sleeping under Hilda's roof!

Last night, after Alicia, in clear frustration, had left the table and her two quarrelsome parents (or one quarrelling parent, to be precise) alone, Hilda's attitude toward him had suddenly softened. They had sat there, him drinking his non-alcoholic beer, Hilda sipping at a glass of red wine.

'I'm so very grateful that I've been able to spend time with Alicia,' Leo had said.

Instead of jumping at his throat as had happened all through the previous two days, Hilda had nodded. There had even been a faint smile playing at the corners of her mouth. Her eyes had become softer too, and at that moment, all Leo could think about was how much he wanted to hold her.

They'd chatted about Alicia, how clever she was, and how competent at running the farm. Hilda had told Leo a little about Uffe, her deceased husband, who by all accounts sounded the perfect partner.

'I'm so sorry for your loss,' Leo had said and he'd placed his hand over Hilda's, which was resting on the table.

To his huge surprise, Hilda had let him hold her for a while like this. Both had been silent, afraid no doubt that the moment would soon fade into another bickering session.

But it hadn't.

Too soon it was time for bed, the evening coming to a close when Hilda began to clear the dishes.

Leo is sad he has to leave already, but at least he feels able to return. He looks at the large clock in the kitchen and realizes that Hilda, who had told him she was going to see how Alicia was doing, has been gone for at least half an hour now. He gets up and decides to investigate what's going on.

'Look, she's busy,' Hilda is saying, holding onto Leo's arm.

They are standing in the middle of Alicia's lounge, which has a stunning view across the reeds toward the open water, with a couple of islands nestling in the distance.

'What is going on?' Leo asks.

'Oh, it's, nothing, really, but I think it best if I take you to the ferry later.'

Leo sees that Hilda is upset. Her eyes are darting back and forth toward the door, and she's biting her lower lip. A habit which he remembers from when they were together. A clear sign that she wasn't telling him everything.

'What's up? You never know, I could help out?'

At that moment, Alicia bursts into the room.

'Oh,' she says when she sees Leo.

As if she's forgotten I'm here.

Alicia gives her mom a look, and Hilda springs into action.

'Would you like another coffee? With a cinnamon bun? I am famous for my baking, you know.'

Leo doesn't reply. He's watching Alicia, who's now pacing across the room, from the door toward the window and back. She looks a bit of a mess, in a frayed pair of jeans and a pale, wrinkled T-shirt.

Afraid he might set Hilda off again, he touches Hilda's arm gently. He chooses his words carefully.

'I'm sorry, but I can't have any sweet things, or milk, or butter, remember? And I've already drunk more coffee than I can manage. But thank you, that's very kind of you.'

While speaking to Hilda, Leo is keeping an eye on his daughter.

'Oh, of course, I forgot.'

Hilda's voice is cool.

'I'm sorry,' Leo says, hoping yet another apology will pacify her.

It seems to do the trick because Hilda nods. They both turn to face their daughter who has come to stand close by.

'Still fighting about the food then?' She says in a sarcastic voice and a manner Leo doesn't recognize.

'No, no, darling, we sorted all that out last night. It was good that you left, wasn't it Leo, so that we could...'

Alicia waves her hand at her mom to stop her talking. She turns on her heels and takes the few paces to the window again. She stays there, looking out to sea.

'You must tell me what the matter is? You are both acting very strangely,' Leo says.

Alicia turns her upper body around and something passes between the two women. His daughter nods to Hilda and she stretches her arm toward the door.

'Let's go into the house and I'll tell you all about it.' Hilda glances at Alicia and adds, 'if that is OK with you, Alicia?'

Alicia is once again facing the windows and doesn't turn around. 'You might as well. He'll know it soon enough, as will the rest of the world.'

CHAPTER FORTY-FOUR

L eo cannot believe his ears. Human trafficking on these islands! In Finland!

'That can't be!'

Hilda gives him a sad smile and nods.

'But I am certain that Uffe wasn't part of it. The article doesn't mention us, or even Sjoland, but we have had Eastern European boys here for many years now. And Uffe did pay them in cash. And they did stay in the cottage over the field.'

Hilda nods her head, indicating the direction of a red building that Leo has seen from the kitchen window. To him, the little house looks idyllic, with its wide sloping roof and a small porch at front.

'But who would write such nonsense?'

'Well, it appears to be true. They have done some research and found this company on the Cayman Islands and a Russian connection.'

Hilda sighs heavily. She's playing with a tissue between her fingers and Leo can see she's close to tears.

'Really?'

Hilda nods.

Her eyes are downcast, and Leo has an irresistible urge to get up and hug her. But, he doesn't dare in case Hilda thinks he's taking advantage of the situation – again. Leo wouldn't want to do that.

He just wants Hilda to be happy. It's making him miserable seeing her like this, despondent. It's so far from what she usually is. Even when talking about her late husband last night, there had been a certain warmth to her voice, her face lighting up when she remembered how they met.

Leo had been jealous, he can admit that to himself, even though he knows the notion is ridiculous. The man has passed, for goodness sake!

'So why not speak with the person who wrote the article? He – or she – might be able to help you, tell you exactly who is involved, or even if Uffe's farm is part of the trafficking ring, or whatever it's called?'

Again, Hilda sighs as if the worries of the world are on her shoulders.

'That's part of the problem. It's Alicia's friend – male friend, or even boyfriend, I guess you could call him.'

'What! Patrick?'

Leo gets up and goes over to the kitchen counter. He never liked that Swedish son of a bitch. He met Patrick once when he was on the islands, before he was dry. He'd been trying to buck up the courage to meet Alicia but had started drinking instead. As usual.

But then he'd bumped into Alicia and Patrick in a

cafe in town. Something about the man had made Leo take an immediate dislike to him. When Patrick returned to the cafe after Alicia had left, and Leo was trying to resist having another beer, his initial reaction to the Swede was vindicated. Patrick had tried to make a deal with him.

'I'll convince Alicia to see you if you say something positive about me.'

Or something like that. Truthfully, Leo can no longer remember what the Swede had said, but it was a sort of 'You scratch my back, I'll scratch yours' kind of proposition.

About his daughter!

His hackles had come up straight away and he remembers telling Patrick if he ever hurt his daughter, he'd have him to deal with him. The Swedish reporter had laughed at Leo's threat, taking it for an empty gesture.

But Leo had meant what he said.

Now keeping his eyes on Hilda, he asks, 'Where's this Swedish journalist's haunt these days? Still in the posh part of Stockholm?'

Hilda gives him a surprised look. Her eyelashes are wet, and once again Leo has to fight the urge to embrace her.

'Why do you ask?'

Hilda dips her head sideways and creases form between her eyebrows.

'I think I should go and see him.'

Hilda opens her mouth, but nothing comes out.

'There's a ferry to Stockholm going at eleven, isn't there? I'll talk to the man and see what he knows. I may even be able to convince him to write another piece in his rag making clear this farm – and your ex-husband – had nothing to do with these nasty rumors.'

CHAPTER FORTY-FIVE

The *Ålandsfärjan* ferry docks at Kapellskär port with a heave and a bang. Hilda turns to look at Leo, sitting next to her in the car. He'd insisted on driving, and she's glad of it, although in normal circumstances she'd be loath to let anyone drive her bright red Mercedes. Today, however, her emotional state is such that she couldn't trust herself behind the wheel.

Her ex-husband on the other hand is filled with energy and determination. Hilda sees the straight line of his mouth and his lips pursed in contained outrage.

After she'd told him all about the article, what Dudnikov had done to her store, and how she'd got to know the Russian through Uffe and Lars, Leo was even more determined to find out the whole story from Patrick. Hilda had suggested phoning or emailing him, but Leo had insisted that surprise was their best weapon.

He actually used the word 'weapon'!

Hilda made only one proviso. She would accompany Leo to Stockholm.

'I know him, Leo. Better than you do. And I know Stockholm.'

For the first time since she still had the shop, before Uffe's death, Hilda felt alive again. She was excited about the prospect of challenging Patrick for what he had done to Alicia.

The more she thought about it, the more she agreed with Leo. Patrick will not expect a visit from her, let alone Leo. He may well crumble under their interrogation.

As they drive along the motorway toward Stockholm, and Hilda sees the countryside fly past her, she smiles to herself. It feels good to do something.

It's been a while since Leo has been in Stockholm, so he's glad of Hilda's knowledge of the city as he navigates the one-way systems and new bridges and roundabouts to Söder and Patrick's new apartment.

When they park on one of the side roads off Mariatorget, Leo gazes out at the tall apartment block where Hilda says Patrick lives.

The area is less fancy than he imagined, although the restaurants and bars are very trendy, and the buildings are beautiful old structures, with delicate windows and rendered walls. It reminds him of Ullanlinna, the old part of Helsinki where he himself lives.

He feels almost at home here, were it not for the

sense of foreboding in his gut. He has a sudden fear that the Swede will laugh in his face.

Leo turns toward Hilda, who is sitting quietly beside him.

'Ready?'

Hilda nods. She reaches over the gearstick and takes hold of Leo's hands.

'Thank you for doing this.'

Her smile gives Leo strength. He releases his seatbelt. 'Let's do this then.'

The apartment is on the top floor, and by the fourth level Hilda is puffing and huffing, so Leo slows down.

'Only one floor to go,' he says, pretending that he, too, is out of breath. But his fitness is so good now, he feels he could have run up the wide staircase. Or perhaps it's his determination to get to the bastard that's stopping him from feeling the exercise.

'How can they have a building with so many floors and no elevator!'

Hilda's exclamation makes Leo smile, but he turns away from Hilda to hide his expression.

Eventually they are standing in front of a door with a sticky tape placed over the letterbox:

Patrick Hilden – No flyers please

'He doesn't want any junk inside his apartment but he's willing to write shit for others to read.'

Hilda points at the writing, but Leo places a hand on her arm.

'Take it easy. We don't want to go there all guns blazing. We want to negotiate, OK?'

Leo has lowered his voice.

'But I thought you said...'

'Yes, but we must keep in mind what our goals are: We need information, and we need his co-operation. The fact that he doesn't expect us, should help us gain an advantage from the start. In the end, we need to come to a mutually agreeable solution.'

'When did you turn into such a wise negotiator?'

There's a smile dancing around Hilda's eyes, a sight that fills Leo's heart with warmth. Again, he wants to take his ex-wife into his arms, but of course this is absolutely not the time. Instead, he rings the bell on the side of the door.

CHAPTER FORTY-SIX

W hen Patrick looks through the spy hole, he cannot believe his eyes.
What the hell?

He thinks for a moment before opening the door. He knew from talking to Alicia that Leo was going to visit the islands, but he'd understood the relationship between her mom and her real father was sticky to say the least.

Didn't Alicia tell him there had been an unresolved rift between her parents from when she was a baby, and that Hilda hadn't wanted to set eyes on her ex since then? So much so that she'd told Alicia her father was dead?

It wasn't until Leo suddenly surfaced last spring that she'd even known of his existence. And now here the two were, cozy as anything outside his door in Stockholm.

Patrick looks down at his tracksuit bottoms and old T-shirt, which he usually wears at home. He runs his fingers through his hair and checks his face briefly in the mirror next to the door. He hasn't shaved yet today, but he'll just have to do.

He opens the door to Hilda and Leo.

'This is a surprise!' Patrick says and tries to raise his lips into a smile.

'Can we come in?' Leo asks.

Neither of the older people are smiling and Patrick senses a hostility he wasn't expecting. He looks at Hilda, but the woman just stands there, her serious eyes steady on him.

'Of course. I'm sorry, I'm not quite presentable. Didn't expect visitors today.'

Patrick gives a forced laugh and stands aside to let them in.

'This is not a social call,' Leo says.

Hilda says nothing. She stands on the floor in the middle of his lounge. Quickly, Patrick removes some books and magazines from a chair and indicates for Hilda to sit. He turns to Leo and points toward the sofa.

'Would you like a drink? Coffee, or something stronger?'

Both Hilda and Leo shake their heads.

He seats himself at his laptop, which he has set in the corner of the room. He shuts it down and turns toward the two visitors.

Before he has time to say anything Hilda exclaims, 'How could you do it!'

Her eyes are wide, with tears pooling inside. To his horror, Patrick realizes she's about to cry.

Leo moves from the chair to sit next to Hilda. He

puts his arm over Hilda's shoulder and says, softly, 'Let me.'

Turning to Patrick, Leo adds, 'What Hilda is trying to say is that we are all very shaken by the article you wrote in your rag, I mean paper.'

Patrick doesn't know what to say. He's been expecting a call from Alicia all day, since five o'clock this morning, when the story was published on the online version of the paper. But there's not been a word from her, which he knows is bad news. But to send her mother and father!

'Didn't Alicia want to come herself to admonish me?'

Too late, Patrick sees that his comment was far too flippant.

Hilda straightens her back, about to say something, and Leo, removing his arm from her shoulders, places his hand in hers, which are clasped in her lap.

Again, Patrick is surprised to see how tight Leo and Hilda are.

'Alicia doesn't know we are here.'

'Oh.'

'This story, with so-called facts affects Alicia, it's true, but it affects Hilda here even more. You are insinuating that Uffe, Hilda's late husband, was involved in something terrible. Something that used young people and forced them into labor for little or no money. We want to see your evidence. If there is black on white to show that Uffe did indeed know, or actively supported people trafficking, which we seriously doubt, we want you to go to the police, not write about it in your trashy rag!'

Patrick can't believe his ears. Is this guy for real?

'Trashy rag? I have to let you know that *Journalen* is one of the oldest newspapers in Sweden, and the most respected.'

'That's beside the point. Do you, or do you not have evidence that Uffe knew about these practices?'

The eyes of the two older people are boring into Patrick. He fiddles with the hem of his overstretched T-shirt.

'No.'

'"No" what?'

Hilda has found her voice and she sounds even angrier than she did standing on his doorstep.

'"No" that my Uffe knew about the boys, or "No" that you don't have any evidence?'

Patrick sighs.

'Look, I didn't see anything about the farm in Sjoland. If that's any consolation to you. But the part of bringing these boys onto the islands to work on farms – that I do have evidence for. I have a diary from a lad from Romania, Daniel, who I believe worked for Uffe? His words tell the story of his passport being taken and not returned to him ... another boy has been in police custody here in Stockholm for some drugs offenses. Same story. Two Russians brought him into the country, and during the summer he worked on the islands. Neither has given any names, but the suspicion is that one of the Russians is a man called Alexander Dudnikov.'

A muffled sound comes out of Hilda and she places a hand over her mouth.

'I'm sorry,' Patrick says.

'What about the company in the Cayman Islands? Who's in charge of that?'

Leo is leaning forward on the sofa, his eyes keenly on Patrick's face.

Patrick has a feeling that the man doesn't like him. He regrets their first meeting, when he had tried to make a deal with him about Alicia. He was not himself that summer on the islands. He and Mia were separating, and he was madly in love with Alicia. He would have done anything, played any dirty trick to get Alicia back.

Alicia.

Patrick can't think about her now. He focuses on his research for the article.

'There is a name. But it belongs to some woman living on the islands. She seems to have nothing to do with any of this. This is the usual practice when you want to hide money from the authorities. The real players are the sleeping partners, who control the company's affairs.'

CHAPTER FORTY-SEVEN

Leo gets up and goes to the open balcony door.

'You have a very nice set-up here, don't you?' He says, turning abruptly around.

Patrick nods. He glances at Hilda, but she seems to be in her own thoughts. Her hands are still clasped together and she's looking down at the floor.

This is not the Hilda Patrick knows and he feels a sudden, painful regret at what he's done. It hadn't occurred to him that his words would have such a profound effect on Uffe's widow too.

All he had thought about was that Alicia would be furious with him and might end their relationship. But Patrick needed to write the article, he needs to make his mark at *Journalen*, and he thought, as a reporter herself, Alicia would understand that.

What have I done?

'But not quite as luxurious as I would have imagined. Isn't this where all the Finns moved to when they emigrated over to Sweden in search of work in the sixties and the seventies?' Leo asks.

Patrick is puzzled by the older man's remark. What is he getting at?

'Yeah, but it's very fashionable now.'

Patrick is answering Leo's questions absentmindedly, while he thinks how he can get himself out of this situation. Perhaps he could write another piece, naming farms other than Uffe's?

But what about Daniel's diary? He went to great lengths not to mention the place in Sjoland as the farm where the boy worked, but surely everyone in Åland would recognize it? Even if Patrick left out descriptions of the cottage and Uffe. Thank goodness he didn't give away the boy's name. That was Axelsson's suggestion.

'We don't want to get the boy's family into trouble, do we? These traffickers are vicious people. They don't think twice about threatening, harming, or even killing a family member. You, too, need to be careful.'

Patrick, to his shame, hadn't even thought about Daniel's family. He'd mentioned his brothers and sister on several occasions in his diary. A cold shiver had run along his spine when Axelsson mentioned his own safety. But surely, that was just the editor's sense of macabre humor at play?

'Didn't you have a much larger place before?'

'What?'

Patrick doesn't understand why Alicia's father is suddenly so interested in his apartment.

'I bet you could use a little more money?'

Patrick doesn't have time to respond before Hilda, now also standing up, asks Leo, 'What are you saying?'

'Yes, what are you going on about?' Patrick asks.

Seeing the expressions on both Leo and Hilda's faces, Patrick realizes that his tone has been wrong again.

'I am trying to make you an offer.'

Leo glances at Hilda, whose eyes are wide, fixed on her ex-husband. Then, he turns toward Patrick and adds, 'So there's no need to be so impertinent, young man.'

Patrick runs his hand through his hair. He needs to think.

Leo returns to the sofa and indicates with his arm for Hilda to follow suit. She remains very subdued, so unlike herself. As if Leo had cast some kind of spell on her, making her lose the ability to speak.

Patrick gazes at his fingers and considers his position.

'You want me to do exactly what?'

He lifts his head to gaze at the couple sitting neatly on the sofa, their backs straight, their eyes peeled on him. Leo is slightly taller than Hilda, but both have serious expressions on their faces. Had they agreed that this is what they'd do? Try to bribe him?

As Patrick waits for a reply, the room remains silent. There's only the sound of some boys shouting loudly to each-other on the street below. A subway train rumbles by, sending slight vibrations through the space.

Finally, Leo speaks.

'You need to retract the article. Convince your editor that you had wrong information, that you had been duped into writing the article. Something like that. I will be able to offer you a substantial amount of money for your co-operation.'

'It will end my career.'

'I said a substantial amount of money,' Leo says.

'Let me get this straight. You want to pay me to retract the article? I'm an honest journalist!'

Leo laughs out loud at Patrick's words.

As if waking up from a daze, Hilda places a hand carefully on Leo's arm and faces Patrick. 'Leo doesn't need to do that. I'm certain Patrick will see that he needs to do what is right without being paid for it!'

Hilda fires a look full of hatred in Patrick's direction.

'As for you. I can say that I have lost even the small amount of respect I had for you. I can't speak for Alicia, but I can assure you, I will do everything in my power to keep you two apart!'

With this, Hilda gets up and turning her face toward Leo says, 'Are you coming?'

CHAPTER FORTY-EIGHT

Alicia has tried to call Lars for hours now. She glances at her phone and realizes it's nearly two o'clock. She promised to take Leo to the ferry, and they should have left by now. Why hasn't he popped his head into her office?

Alicia gets up and runs across the yard to the main house. She's surprised to see the door is closed. Hilda must have taken Leo herself. She dials her mom's cell number and waits for an answer.

'Are you in town? I'm so sorry, I completely forgot about Leo. Is he OK? Did he make the ferry?'

Hilda sounds out of breath when she answers.

'Yes, he's fine. He's with me. No need to worry.'

Alicia looks at the display on her cell and sees it's now five past two.

'I don't understand. The ferry should have left for Helsinki by now.'

Hilda gives a little awkward laugh.

'There was a change of plan. We're in Stockholm, but

we're just about to take the *Ålandsfärjän* back. We must rush now, darling. Everything is absolutely fine. We'll see you back at home.'

With that Hilda ends the call.

What is going on?

Alicia stands in the middle of the yard, next to the beautiful round flower bed, where Hilda's roses are in full bloom. She cannot understand why Hilda and Leo would be together. And in Stockholm. She shakes her head. She hasn't got the headspace to deal with her warring parents now.

CHAPTER FORTY-NINE

The newspaper office is empty this early on a Monday morning. The cleaners are still there, and Patrick nods and wishes a young woman 'Good Morning'. She smiles but doesn't reply; she just bends her head down and continues to work the floor with a polishing machine.

Patrick thinks about what he learned from Daniel's diary about the cleaning jobs they did in Stockholm. Who is to know whether this woman is also a modern-day slave? He makes a mental note to mention this to Axelsson. The company he'd found in the Cayman Islands had connections to several firms in Stockholm, but Axelsson had cut most of the references to Sweden from the article. Which Patrick thought was highly unprofessional.

Reading the feature, you got the idea that Åland was the center of the people trafficking activities, when in truth, Patrick knows it's just a sideshow. According to Daniel, and the boy in custody in Stockholm, working on the island farms was a bit like a reward for good behavior during the horrible winters in the Swedish Capital.

Of course, he knew all this.

His ego got the better of him. He should have kept to his previous promise to himself – not to chase stupid dreams of journalistic fame. It's clear now that Axelsson took advantage of his weakness for recognition.

Why does Patrick need such acclamation? Let's face it, he's a good journalist, but not a brilliant one. He's also not keen on playing the game; he hates the in-crowd of journalists, who pretend to be so worthy, when all they are thinking about is how to advance their own careers.

When he was with Mia, they attended a lot of events where he had the opportunity to meet important people. Since their divorce, he's avoided those circles. Who'd want to go out and keep bumping into their ex?

He hasn't wanted to go near Mia unless it's to collect the girls – something he rarely does these days because they can travel on their own. That way, he doesn't have to tell Alicia about seeing Mia.

Since his terrible mistake last year, Mia's name alone brings a chill to his relationship with Alicia. Patrick is sincerely sorry about his actions, and he can see that Alicia has great difficulty forgetting them. He doesn't think she's fully forgiven him, and now he's done something even more stupid.

Seeing and listening to Hilda and Leo has made Patrick's mind up. It's time to move on. But first he needs to do something about the storm he has created.

CHAPTER FIFTY

Alicia drives toward Mariehamn. She's been trying to get in touch with her farm manager all morning, but her messages have gone unanswered and her phone calls to voicemail. Although it's Sunday, she decides to drive to his house in Östernäs, in the southeastern part of the city. She's been to his two-bedroom house once before, when his car hadn't started on an unusually frosty May morning.

Lars had lived on his own since his wife died a few years before, and she'd been surprised how modern and expensive-looking the furniture had been. He'd offered her a coffee while she waited for him to call a mechanic. The floors were polished dark wood, the walls a modern greenish-gray and the three-piece suite appeared brand-new, as did the large standard lamps either side of the couch.

There was even an oriental rug in the middle of the room. The whole decor reminded Alicia of a posh club in London's Soho, rather than a small bungalow on the islands. It was certainly not stuff bought from IKEA.

'Have you remodelled the house recently?' Alicia had asked.

Lars's reaction had surprised her at the time. A deep red color had risen in his cheeks and he'd stammered his reply. He was holding his cell to his ear, waiting for the car repair guy to answer.

'Hmm, yes, well, my wife had a policy, what do you call them, life assurance. I had no idea what to do here, so I got in an interior designer from Stockholm.'

At that point, his call was answered and soon they were on their way to Sjoland in Alicia's Volvo.

Alicia hadn't mentioned the house to Lars since, thinking that he was still missing his wife, and that was the reason her question had flustered him.

But now, her suspicions rising, she is wondering where all the money for the expensive makeover had come from.

Lars also had his villa in Spain.

The way he described it, there was quite a bit of land included in the property. Again, Alicia had wondered, absentmindedly, how a farm manager could afford a second home abroad, but she hadn't thought much about it. Now a fear is rising in her gut, as it has done all morning.

Alicia turns into Salstigen and stops by the white bungalow with its sloping tiled roof and two square windows. There is greenery at the front of the house, including a large bush at the entrance hiding it from the road. Alicia steps out of her car and goes to ring the bell.

She waits for a few minutes and tries again. The house seems quiet, so Alicia steps to the side to look through one of the windows.

'Gone away!' Somebody shouts behind her.

A woman is standing on the opposite side of the road, leaning on the roof of her battered red Ford Fiesta. She has her car keys in her hand and a large canvas bag slung across her shoulder.

'Do you know when he left, or where he might have gone?'

'Well,' the woman regards Alicia with suspicion.

'Sorry, I'm Alicia O'Connell from Ulsson's farm in Sjoland. Lars works with me.'

'You're the Ulssons' girl. I thought I recognized you!'

The woman walks around her car and comes over to Alicia, stretching out her hand.

'Tove Holm. I live there,' she jerks her head toward the house opposite, which is in considerably worse repair than Lars's property. When Alicia looks around, she notices that many of the houses have chipped paint or unkempt front gardens.

'I have a baby. She woke early and that's when I saw Lars with a suitcase – well, two very large cases – getting into his car. I assumed he was off on vacation. Didn't he tell you he was taking time off?'

Alicia thanks the woman and assures her that she'd forgotten about Lars's vacation.

On her way back to Sjoland, past the Eastern Harbor and *Gräddhyllan*, where Brit and Jukka live, she thinks back to how Lars has behaved since she took over the farm. How insistent he'd been on taking on the East

European boys. How he had pressurized her to make a decision. She'd thought he was thinking about what was best for the farm, but now she wonders about his real motivation.

Back at home Alicia goes to her office and opens up her computer. She sends an email to the woman who has been doing Uffe's accounts for as long as she can remember. There must be some trail to tell her how payments to the labor agent were handled. And by whom.

CHAPTER FIFTY-ONE

L ater that day, Alicia is on the phone to the accountant, or rather her assistant, a young man, who seems to have no information whatsoever.

'Is Disa in the office today? I want to come and see her,' she's saying when she hears a knock on her front door.

'It's open!' She shouts, and says to the man on the phone, 'I'll see you at 10am.'

Without waiting for a reply, she turns around. She's expecting to see Leo. Her mom wouldn't knock if she saw that the door was open. But instead of her father, to her shock, Patrick is standing in the doorway.

His physical presence still makes Alicia's tummy flutter. Even when he is the last person on earth she wants to see right now, she can't help that the sight of his white T-shirt straining over his muscular frame, makes her feel dizzy. But she controls herself.

'What are you doing here?'

Patrick takes a step toward her, but Alicia puts her hand up.

'How dare you turn up like this?'

She's trying to keep her voice level, but she can still hear a tremble in it.

'Alicia,' Patrick says and her heart melts a little.

His hands are outstretched with the palms up and his eyes are pleading with her.

'What did you think would happen when you wrote a story about my farm? About my dear, late, stepfather's pride and joy? A farm that has been handed down for three generations. What did you think a story like that would do to me, let alone to Hilda? On this gossip-ridden island? And not only that, why didn't you warn me? Now I've not only lost my reputation, but I've also lost my farm manager!'

'What? Why? You mean Lars? What does he have to do with anything?'

Alicia sighs.

'I'm not sure to be honest, but he's disappeared. He left early this morning, which is highly suspicious.'

Alicia looks back at her computer, where she's trying to find out about Lars's financial situation.

In Finland, everyone's income is detailed in the country's tax records online, but all Alicia can see from his last return is his meager salary from the Ulsson's farm.

The house in Östernäs is only worth 75,000 Euros and he has no other assets. The property in Spain isn't listed. Could he be renting it each time he goes there? He spoke about it as though he owned it, but Alicia cannot be certain.

If he does own it, why isn't it listed on his tax return? And if he rents, how can he afford it on his salary?

Patrick is standing behind her. She turns around and their faces are so close she can see he's cut himself shaving again. Involuntarily, she smiles.

Patrick notices Alicia's expression and says softly, 'You've no idea how truly sorry I am. It was my stupid ambition, and Axelsson. He changed the article to make it seem as if Åland is the center of the trafficking when it's all run in Stockholm.'

Patrick leans into her for a kiss.

Alicia puts her hand up and glares at Patrick.

'Don't you dare! And don't put this on your bloody editor. You know what he's like. You wrote the piece and pressed send!'

Patrick gets up and Alicia, who's turned back toward her screen, hears him sigh deeply.

'What can I do to make it better?'

CHAPTER FIFTY-TWO

When Patrick tells Alicia what he has done, she isn't certain she can believe her ears.

'You've resigned? Are you sure?'

Patrick nods.

They are sitting opposite each other in Alicia's office. The sun is streaming in through the window behind Patrick, giving his blond hair a strange-looking halo. Alicia snorts out loud.

As if he was any kind of saint.

Patrick thinks her reaction is to do with his job and his eyebrows shoot up.

'I thought you'd be pleased. I can now come back to the islands, live here and be close to you.'

Alicia nearly laughs out loud.

The guy has a nerve.

Their relationship had been sliding down the plughole even before he betrayed her with the article. During the past five months, they've barely seen each other. And when they do, they often end up arguing.

It's been difficult for Alicia to leave the farm, for obvious reasons, and Patrick hasn't wanted to compromise on his career at *Journalen*. Something that Alicia totally understood.

However, even their daily phone calls have dried up in the past month. They just don't seem to have anything in common anymore. Alicia has been wondering if their relationship is so strongly based on sex, that it can't survive a distance.

Their physical closeness has always been amazing, and the pillar on which their relationship has been built. At first, when they were living apart, with a whole sea between them, Alicia had found it hard and had wanted to speak to Patrick several times a day. But soon, she began to resent his absence, and she hated being a needy girlfriend.

She had steeled herself and concentrated on running the farm, learning what she needed to do and working with Lars to carry on where Uffe had left off. Now, with everything that has happened, how could Patrick think they can go back in time?

'And what makes you think that's what I want?'

'Please, Alicia, you know what a stupid man I can be. I need you to hold me together. To pin my feet to the ground.'

As if to demonstrate, Patrick gets up and comes to kneel next to her.

'Patrick, get up. I don't have time for this now.'

'But I love you.'

Patrick takes Alicia's hand in his.

Alicia pulls herself away and waves her hand at him.

She turns her head toward the door. She doesn't want to look at him.

How can he say that now?

She can hear Patrick get up and walk toward the window. With his back to her, he begins to speak.

'Early this morning, I posted a correction, refuting all the information. I said I had been fed false facts. I don't think Axelsson will print my retraction, but I've posted it on my blog and shared it widely on social media.'

Alicia turns around at the same time as Patrick. They stare at each other. Alicia takes in the sincere expression on his face. There's not a hint of the smile that usually hovers around the corners of his mouth.

'I want to make this go away.'

Alicia gazes at him for a moment longer and then makes a decision.

'Since you are here, you might as well help me.'

CHAPTER FIFTY-THREE

'Uffe's accountant – or rather her assistant – sent over all the accounts from the last five years. I've been trying to go through them, but I haven't found anything unusual.'

Alicia sighs and rubs the bridge of her nose.

'OK,' Patrick says, then carefully, gazing at Alicia, he makes a suggestion. 'Have you looked at the files from the agency that you told me organizes the labor? Could there be anything there?'

As he had feared, Alicia gives him an annoyed look.

'Of course I have,' she says tightly.

She tells Patrick that the company is incorporated in Stockholm and seems to be above board. She shows him the listing on the Swedish company registry site.

Patrick taps the address information onto the map app on his cell.

'That's strange,' he says.

'What?'

Alicia leans over him, making his pulse quicken. The

place where the labor agency is supposed to be situated is a communal swimming pool.

Alicia's eyes meet Patrick's. 'That's not right. I'm going to look at the bank account details.'

After a lot of digging and calculations, Alicia and Patrick find that the company has been paid a whopping 50,000 Euros each year for seasonal labor from Uffe's farm account.

'That's more than ten times the cost Lars gave me! And it's been allocated wrongly into various headings in the accounts.'

'It looks as if the arrangement has been going on for nearly twenty years. Look,' Patrick points at the screen. 'On the company's ledger, it says the details were entered in 2002. The total turnover of invoices issued to the farm is over a million Euros!'

Alicia and Patrick stare at the screen for a moment.

'How could Uffe not have known about this?'

As Alicia turns her face toward Patrick, he sees she's unusually pale. Then her face hardens. 'Let's see where all the money went.'

After more digging, they find that all the payments were made to the same account in the Cayman Islands. Alicia decides to look into all the payments made from Uffe's farm account. They find that labor charges against several other farms on the islands have been paid into the same account in the Cayman Islands. And that two other companies are using the same payment details – one a company providing tractor repairs and the other supplying computer software. Both have been paid large amounts from Uffe's bank account, although much less and more sporadically than to the labor agency.

'Look,' Alicia exclaims. 'The labor charges for several farms around here have gone through Uffe's accounts!'

Patrick looks at Alicia.

'I tried to talk to the other farmers but they wouldn't take my calls.'

Alicia glances at Patrick. Her face is set in stone.

'I know.'

Patrick's eyebrows shoot up.

'How?'

'It's a small community,' Alicia replies, adding, 'Uffe didn't even have a computer! And as for tractor repairs, Uffe and Lars used to look after the one machine themselves. I can't ever remember it being taken to a repair shop.'

'Do you know who signed off the bills?'

Patrick is gazing at Alicia. He can see half of her face, illuminated by the glare from her computer screen. There's worry etched onto her features and he feels ashamed of himself.

What is career success if it loses you the love of your life?

'Look, I'm so sorry,' he says, putting his hand on Alicia's fingers, which are on the mouse.

Alicia turns to face him, but instead of looking at him, she has her eyes on Patrick's hand covering hers. He removes it and sighs.

'I don't know what came over me. Axelsson insisted I

was the perfect person to write about the islands, and I guess I am. But I just didn't think.'

'Yes, that's exactly right. You didn't think.'

Alicia's eyes when she lifts them up at him are stern.

'But we don't have the time to talk about that now. I'm going to see Uffe's lawyer and accountant in town. I want Disa to explain to me how hundreds of thousands of Euros have been paid out of Uffe's farm account into a bogus bank account in the Cayman Islands. You coming?'

Just as they are about to leave, Alicia's cell rings. She speaks on the telephone for a moment, all the while looking at Patrick. He can't decipher her mood, so he stays silent.

'That was Ebba. She wants to see us – both of us.'

licia and Patrick are stopped in the yard by Hilda. She's standing at the door to the main house.

'You two! Come inside!'

Patrick gives Alicia a sheepish look.

'I'm not her favorite person at the moment.'

Alicia can't believe the conspiratorial tone of his voice.

When Hilda and Leo returned from Stockholm the night before, they told Alicia all about their visit to see Patrick. Alicia had been astonished. But not as surprised as she had been when Hilda told her that Leo had tried to buy Patrick off.

'What?'

Leo had looked very ashamed of himself.

'I panicked,' he said, gazing at Hilda, who was standing with her arms crossed over her chest.

'Luckily Patrick wouldn't hear of it. It seems he has

some integrity left. But I do think that Leo's offer made him see how seriously we took the situation.'

'I bet,' Alicia had murmured and hid a smile that had formed on her lips.

'I know all about their visit. Serves you right,' Alicia now says and walks toward the house.

She doesn't care if Patrick follows or not. She does, however, want him to go with her to the lawyer's office, as well as to see the accountant and the police chief. She wants to make sure Patrick sees how little Uffe was involved in any illegal activity. Having been through the books, and not being able to get hold of Lars, has convinced her that her mild-mannered stepfather knew nothing about the boys. Or their horrible fate.

She hears a deep sigh behind her, and Patrick falls in line with her.

'Have you two had anything to eat?'

'Mom, we're about to go into town to see Old Ledin.'

It's what Uffe used to call his lawyer, even though the two of them were the same age and had been to school together in Mariehamn. She smiles at her father and goes to hug him.

'You OK to stay a few more days, Leo?'

Alicia raises her eyebrows and nods toward her mom, who is bringing a large plate to the table. She places it down and goes back to the kitchen cabinets.

With her back to everyone, she says, 'That's a great idea, but you also need to eat. I've made some open sandwiches. There's salmon, ham and cheese. And coffee, naturally.'

Alicia looks at the spread on the kitchen table. In addition to the large plateful of rye and wheat sandwiches, there's also a stack of freshly baked cinnamon buns. She glances behind her at Patrick, who's still standing in the hall.

CHAPTER FIFTY-FIVE

'Come in, Patrick,' Hilda says.

Her tone is neutral, and she's not smiling. But when it comes to food, Hilda would feed an invading army. As long as they appreciated the food.

Nodding to Leo, Patrick sits at the table, and coughs into his hand.

'This is very kind of you,' he says, addressing Hilda.

Alicia's mom turns. 'Not at all,' she says tightly.

'So have you found out anything?'

'Well, yes,' Alicia says. She looks at her mom, assessing how much she should say without upsetting her. Hilda's face is open, her eyebrows high, waiting for a reply, so Alicia continues.

'We found that huge sums had been paid into a bank account in the Cayman Islands.

'What?'

Her mom is in the middle of dishing out. She stops with an open sandwich held in mid-air. It's piled high with lettuce, smoked salmon and cucumber, topped with a dollop of mayonnaise and crowned with a bunch of dill. Alicia is afraid that any minute now her mom is going to drop it straight into Patrick's lap.

Would serve him right!

'Mom, put that down and I'll tell you!'

'Ah,' Hilda says and places the sandwich on Patrick's plate.

Alicia tells Hilda and Leo about the sums of money and the seemingly fake invoices.

'I can't help thinking that Lars suddenly leaving the country and not answering his phone have something to do with all this,' Patrick says.

Hilda regards him for a moment but doesn't say anything. Instead, she turns to Alicia.

'Is that what you think too?'

Alicia is quiet for a moment before saying anything. Hilda has known Lars for years, probably decades. Uffe trusted him implicitly, and they both saw him almost every day. He was like family. Would he have been able to con them so fundamentally?

'I don't know,' Alicia says and continues, 'But I just want to get hold of him. He was supposed to go on vacation after the harvest was over, not now. And even if he got the days mixed up, why not tell me? Or answer his phone. Now when I try to call it, there's just a long sound as if the number is disconnected. I have to admit, Mom, it's very suspicious.'

Hilda nods several times, pressing her lips together and gazing down at the table.

'And you think Old Ledin might be able to help us find out if it's true?'

'No,' Alicia replies.

She takes a bite out of the corner of a cheese sandwich, equally laden with ingredients. A coffee house in Stockholm would be proud of a spread like this, she thinks.

'He called me earlier. I guess he'd seen the papers.' Alicia gives Patrick a look, which is met with another sheepish glance.

'Who we really want to see is Disa Kello, you know, Uffe's bookkeeper. She should be able to show us the invoices. We want to see who signed them off.'

'Oh.'

Hilda's hand flies to her mouth.

'You don't think?'

She doesn't have to finish the sentence.

'Mom, I really cannot believe Dad had anything to do with this.'

Alicia realizes she's used that word, *Dad*, for Uffe, and turns toward Leo.

But her birth father lifts his hand up and says, 'I know he was a father to you.'

'Thank you. I do miss him terribly, especially now.'

Alicia can feel a lump in her throat, and she looks down at her clasped hands in her lap, her nails pressing into the palms.

The sadness always takes her by surprise. It surfaces at the most unexpected moments. And at the most inconvenient ones.

'Me too,' Hilda says and comes over to hug Alicia.

Alicia tries to control herself and manages to stop the tears before they surface. She can see from the corner of her eyes that the two men, Leo and Patrick, glance at each other.

What is it about men and women's tears, she thinks, and the thought enables her to pull herself together.

She needs to be strong. Strong for Uffe and for her mother. She needs to prove that her late stepfather had nothing whatsoever to do with the people trafficking. Or rather, that he absolutely didn't know how the poor boys had been used.

Alicia frees herself from her mother's embrace. She smiles at Hilda.

'Sorry, I'm not sure what came over me. I'm OK now. What I wanted to say is that I believe that Lars signed those invoices and that the payments were made into his account.

We found another two companies that had the same bank details. That's classic fraud. You make up false invoices and pay them to yourself. I just need to know if Disa knew or had any suspicions about it. Or indeed Lars Olen.'

CHAPTER FIFTY-SIX

E bba is surprised to see Alicia seemingly on good terms with Patrick. She would have thought that an article accusing her stepfather of involvement in modern-day slavery would have put an end to their already fractious relationship.

Alicia and Ebba have formed a friendship since Jabulani moved to the islands and Ebba had come out. Alicia has been a great support to her and one of the few people who weren't in any way judgmental about Ebba's sexual orientation. When Ebba and Jabulani moved in together, Alicia had been genuinely happy for them both. Since then, they have been out for lunch or a drink together, when Ebba's schedule allows. Which isn't often.

Ebba sighs. Only that morning Jabulani had hinted at going to stay with a friend in Stockholm next weekend.

'It's a bit lonely for me when you're always at work,' she said.

It was a conversation they had had far too many times in the past few months.

Sunday was another day when Ebba wasn't supposed to be on duty but had been forced to change her shift at the last minute. The damned budget cuts were affecting all their personal lives in the Åland police force. Besides, she wanted to investigate the allegations made in the *Journalen* herself.

Yesterday, Ebba had received several phone calls about the report. One was from Kurt Eriksson himself, who demanded that 'the reputation of the islands as a fair and decent society' be restored. It had been at the tip of Ebba's tongue to tell the arrogant millionaire that it was his own son-in-law who had written the article.

The editor of *Journalen*, as far as Ebba knew, was also Kurt's personal friend. Why wasn't he aware of the story before it was printed? And with his not inconsiderable influence, why couldn't he get the Swedish paper to pull the story and issue an apology to the islanders?

Another unwelcome call came from the Governor of the Islands. Ebba had only spoken to the man once before, when she was appointed. She certainly doesn't want to repeat the experience of their brief conversation earlier that morning ever again. He'd told her in no uncertain terms that Ebba needed to make sure the allegations made by Patrick could be refuted, 'completely and decisively, with the utmost urgency'.

CHAPTER FIFTY-SEVEN

'Hello Alicia.'

Ebba stands up from behind her desk and hugs her friend. She lets go and nods at Patrick, who's standing behind Alicia. He has a satchel slung across his chest. He didn't want to come and see the police chief, but Alicia hadn't given him a choice.

'Please sit,' Ebba says and points to two chairs placed at an angle on the other side of her desk.

There is a silence while Ebba stares at Patrick.

'A fine mess you've got us all into. Was it worth it?'

Patrick's head is hanging. He looks like an admonished puppy. In any other situation, Alicia would find his demeanor funny, even endearing, but now she is just furious with him.

'I've had the Governor and Kurt Eriksson on the phone. Neither conversation was a particularly pleasant one.'

Ebba's eyes are resting on Patrick, but he's still not

saying a word. He shifts on his seat, and gives a quick glance in Alicia's direction, as if appealing for help.

The man is unreal.

'Thanks to you, I am launching a widespread investigation into your allegations. It will take a lot of police hours, spending our valuable and scarce resources. I hope to God you have done your research properly and we will find something. Of course, there are many parts of this society who will want us to find nothing, but now we have no choice but to look into the matter. I hope you're happy.'

'Do you think you'll find something?'

Alicia can hear the tremble in her own voice.

Ebba turns her head toward Alicia and, taking a softer tone, says, 'To be truthful, I don't know. I don't want to jeopardize the investigation with my own suspicions or the lack of them.'

The police chief sighs and looks at Patrick once again. 'There is also the issue of Daniel's missing diary. I believe that is the diary you quoted from in the story?'

At last Patrick speaks.

'I can't reveal my sources.'

Ebba stares at him and Alicia is glad of the police chief's wrath. It's what Patrick deserves.

'We'll see about that.'

'And I've issued a retraction, making it clear all the information I had was hearsay.'

Alicia ignores Patrick and tells Ebba in detail what they have found out about her farm manager, Lars, and the accountant, Disa.

'Neither can be found at home and I suspect they've

left the islands. We managed to get into Disa's office because there was a young guy there. A summer intern, I think. He gave us all the paperwork. Looking at the farm accounts, it seems that Lars and Disa have co-operated in creating false invoices and paying themselves vast sums over the years. It seems to hang together with the Eastern European labor somehow, but we can't really piece together how the boys were supplied. Or by whom.'

'OK, I'll put out a search warrant for both. Disa Kello and Lars Olen. You wouldn't have their personal ID number on you, would you?'

Ebba is typing on her computer, while Alicia digs in her file. She finds Lars's personnel details but not Disa's.'

'All I have is Disa's company registration number.'

Ebba takes the papers from Alicia and continues to tap quickly on her keyboard.

Alicia glances sideways at Patrick, who gives her a grin. She turns her eyes back to the police chief while shaking her head. Does he not understand the severity of the situation? For everyone living on these islands.

After issuing search warrants for Alicia's farm manager and accountant to the Finnish and Swedish police, Europol, and Interpol, Ebba is quiet.

Her thoughts return to the dead boy's diary. If it wasn't for the mistake they made in not recording the diary as one of the items found in the cottage in Sjoland, she could take Patrick right down to the cells now. Which she has a good mind to do anyway. But she knows it would look very bad and make the situation even worse. She can see the headlines.

Åland Police arrests journalist who revealed slavery on the islands

That would be a gift to the newspapers and the online gossipmongers.

But Patrick doesn't know that the police have no record of the diary.

At that moment, Ebba hears commotion outside her door, which suddenly bursts open.

CHAPTER FIFTY-EIGHT

'I'm sorry, he just barged in.'

The young female police officer looks abashed.

At the door stands Andrei Tamas.

He's wearing the clothes he wore when he came to see Ebba a couple of days ago. His hair is messy, and he has a pronounced stubble on his chin and around his mouth.

Ebba glances briefly at Alicia and Patrick and decides that Andrei's presence might be a good thing.

'Don't worry. I needed to see Mr Tamas anyway.'

'Come in,' Ebba adds, addressing Daniel's brother.

She asks the policewoman to fetch another seat.

Andrei steps inside the room and nods to Alicia.

Ebba also gets to her feet and goes to shake Andrei Tamas's hand. To her dismay, she sees his eyes are bloodshot and there's a scent of alcohol. Is the boy inebriated? Or just hungover?

'I am finished waiting. You tell me now what happen

to my brother!'

The young man spits out the words.

'Meet Patrick. He's a Swedish journalist who knows more about your brother than any of us,' Ebba says in English.

Andrei's gaze lands on Patrick, who before giving Ebba a hateful glance, also rises and stretches out his hand.

But before the Romanian has time to shake hands with Patrick the policewoman returns with a chair and everyone sits back down.

'Is that all, Ebba?'

The new policy of calling everyone in the force by their first name still grates on the police chief, so Ebba doesn't reply, but flicks her hand to show the police-woman that she is no longer needed. At least old Rönngren still shows her some respect, she thinks.

When the young man has settled down, Alicia turns to him and asks in English, 'How are you, Andrei?'

Ebba thinks that Alicia is trying to find out whether he knows about the article.

Andrei smiles at Alicia and replies, 'OK.'

From his response Ebba concludes that he hasn't yet read the papers. Or that the story has not hit the international headlines yet. Perhaps it never will.

Why then, has Andrei been drinking?

He must be missing his brother, Ebba thinks and admonishes herself for being so judgmental. Although, that is her job.

'I believe Patrick has something that belonged to your brother,' Ebba says.

Alicia and Patrick look at her. Alicia's mouth opens, but she doesn't say anything. She then gives Patrick a look, which Ebba has difficulty interpreting. Is Alicia at last beginning to get angry at her boyfriend?

'You do know that stealing evidence carries a severe sentence?'

Ebba can see from the way the journalist's face pales that he hadn't thought of that.

'As I said, I can't reveal my sources.'

Guilty as charged.

'I don't understand,' Alicia says.

Andrei, too, looks puzzled.

'What evidence?' he asks, moving his eyes from Ebba to Patrick.

Ebba ignores Andrei and Patrick but, still speaking in English for Andrei's benefit, addresses Alicia.

'Patrick stole a piece of evidence, namely Daniel's diary. Do you remember when you looked through material in my office after Daniel's body was found? Well, the famous investigative journalist here took the diary.'

Alicia's mouth opens and closes again, without uttering a sound. She turns to stare at Patrick, who has his head bent down.

'What!' Andrei gets up, and for a moment Ebba regrets her snap decision to let the boy in.

'Please sit down, she says, adding, 'Remember where you are.'

Andrei stares at her for a moment but, glaring at Patrick, sits back down. His look makes Patrick visibly uncomfortable, and he shifts on his seat.

'You can't prove that it was Daniel's diary quoted in

the article.'

Patrick is staring at his hands, which are resting on his lap.

'Oh, can't I? You just wait.'

Ebba rises from her seat. She's had enough of this game.

Andrei, too, rises and goes to stand close to Patrick.

'You give diary to me!'

Patrick stands up and puts both hands up, his palms facing outward.

'I don't have it, I swear.'

Now Alicia finally finds her voice and says, 'Yes you do.'

Turning to Andrei, she adds, 'You should have it.'

Ebba decides she needs to intervene. The Romanian looks ready to pounce on Patrick, and that just won't do. If he's still drunk, he will be much more volatile. She gets up and, touching Andrei's arm, speaks with authority.

'I have all Daniel's items, apart from the diary.'

Here Ebba moves her gaze from Andrei to Patrick, and back again. 'Would you like them?'

The Romanian nods. He is still staring at Patrick.

Ebba opens the door to her office and calls the duty policewoman.

'Can you please get all the evidence material taken from Mr Daniel Tamas's home and give it to his brother.'

The policewoman gazes at Andrei with visible suspicion but replies, 'Of course, follow me.'

Reluctantly, it seems, Andrei steps out of the room and follows the policewoman.

CHAPTER FIFTY-NINE

When the door has closed behind Andrei, Ebba says, 'Now, I must ask you also to leave.'

She doesn't extend her hand to shake either of theirs, but just indicates the door with her outstretched arm.

Patrick rises quickly, and glancing toward Alicia, waits for her to follow him.

'Ebba, could I have a quick word?'

Ebba nods to Alicia and looks at Patrick, making it clear she wants him out of her office.

The man lifts his satchel from the floor and places it over his head. He takes the few steps to the door, and before closing it behind him, says to Alicia, 'I'll wait outside.'

She nods and sits back down.

'Sorry to take more of your time, but I have to know something.'

Ebba sighs again.

'OK, shoot.'

'Do you think Dudnikov is really behind all of this?'

Ebba's mouth is in a straight line. She regards Alicia for a moment before replying.

'That would be my best guess. But if you two couldn't find a mention of his name in connection with the Sjoland farm, and Patrick didn't uncover anything during his research, I doubt whether we'll find anything.'

'But you were going to arrest him last spring?'

'True, but I was going on a whim that he had acted illegally here. I had no real evidence, remember? Only the arrest warrant from Sweden.'

Ebba leans toward Alicia and takes her hands into hers.

'Look, he is well and truly out of the picture now. Coming so close to being arrested, even if we had nothing to keep him for longer than the allotted time, would have made life very uncomfortable for him in his circles. The Russian mafia doesn't take many risks when it comes to the authorities. In Finland, we are pretty incorruptible, so if there was evidence, he would have gone to jail.'

Alicia looks puzzled.

'What about this investigation you are going to carry out into what Patrick claimed in his article. Surely you will unearth something.'

Again, the police chief sighs.

'I wish I had your confidence in the police force's capabilities.'

Ebba leans back in her chair and lets go of Alicia's hands.

'Don't tell this to your boyfriend ...'

Alicia interrupts Ebba.

'I'm not sure Patrick qualifies as that anymore.'

Her friend's eyebrows rise.

'I don't want to tell you what to do, but I think that might be a wise decision.'

Thinking about breaking it off with Patrick and hearing it from her good, no-nonsense police friend, makes the separation more realistic. Can she do it?

'I'm sorry, I didn't mean to meddle.'

Ebba sounds so concerned that Alicia tries to smile.

'It's OK. You're only saying what I'm thinking.'

CHAPTER SIXTY

When Patrick steps out of the police station, he spots the Romanian smoking a cigarette. He hasn't seen him, so Patrick walks briskly in the opposite direction from the younger man. Then he hears steps behind him, and a hand on his shoulder.

'You!'

'Let go of me!' Patrick says.

Daniel's brother drops his hand, but his face and body are full of aggression.

'What do you want?'

Patrick is trying to sound neutral, so as not to arouse the guy's anger any further.

But the Romanian doesn't reply. The two men stand facing each other.

A woman pulling a shopping cart with wheels walks past, giving them a quizzical look. Seeing that the street is fairly busy calms Patrick down a little. Surely the Romanian wouldn't attack him here in bright daylight?

'Give me the diary. Now!'

Andrei Tamas is slightly taller than Patrick and certainly in better shape than he is. Muscles are bulging inside his T-shirt.

'What makes you think I have it?'

The Romanian steps even closer to Patrick. His bloodshot eyes are threatening and Patrick swallows hard.

'OK, OK.'

Patrick digs inside his satchel and gets out the black ringed diary, which he'd stolen from the evidence material just as Ebba said. He realizes that not having it in his possession might be the best thing. That way, the police chief will not be able to bring charges. Somehow, he doubts whether she'd do it anyway. Surely, she would have already proceeded, if she could?

Perhaps it was too much hassle and would just have reopened the investigation into Daniel's death? He's sure the police chief would not have wanted that.

Patrick knows how the islanders like to keep the peace and dislike any kind of publicity, be it good or bad.

Andrei snatches the book from Patrick's hands and holds it in both of his. When he looks back up at Patrick, he can see tears in the Romanian's eyes.

'Thank you,' he says.

CHAPTER SIXTY-ONE

F rida buys the local paper from a kiosk on her
way to pick up Anne Sofie from the nursery. It's
something she's been doing since she enrolled
her daughter at the pre-school place. It's quaintly old-
fashioned to be reading a physical copy of a paper, but
she remembers her mom doing it, and carrying on the
tradition makes her feel close to her.

She's early, so she sits on a bench by the market
square and begins shifting through the articles. The
headline immediately grabs her attention.

**Russian gang people trafficking farm labor to
Åland**

Frida drops the paper, and a shriek comes out of her
mouth. An elderly man sitting next to her turns his head
and stares at Frida.

'Everything alright, dear?'

Frida nods to the man and manages a faint smile. She
picks up the paper again and forces herself to read the

whole piece. She sees that the story refers to an article written by Patrick in *Journalen*.

Of all people!

Her first thoughts go to Alicia. Daniel worked at the farm in Sjoland, so surely it is implicated? As she reads on, she sees that no names are mentioned.

Frida is aware that many East European boys are working on farms all over the islands, but since Patrick is involved with Alicia, it seems highly likely, the story has its source there.

Then something else hits her like a heavy weight placed on her chest. It can't be! Is it Daniel's diary that Patrick is quoting from in the article?

She knows she must tell Andrei about the story, unless he's already seen it. No, he would not know about it. Frida gets her cell out and finds the original piece in the Swedish paper online.

It was only published yesterday, so it's unlikely it would have hit any of the news channels abroad. It will most likely not even meet the news threshold. A few Eastern European boys suspected of being used as slave labor on a small Scandinavian island is hardly world news.

But to Frida it is.

And for Andrei.

What is she going to do?

The author of the diary and the other unidentified boy Patrick has been interviewing mention two Russians who controlled their every move.

They took my passport and never gave it back.

We had little or no food and very little pay. There were many, many of us. Every year, new boys would come.

Frida plays with her hair, placing a few strands in her mouth. This is a new habit she's formed since her short spiky hair has grown. She knows it's silly but sucking on her own hair calms her down.

She suspects she knows who at least one of these Russians is.

Her father.

Is that where the money came from?

She thinks what it would mean to lose all the money her mother left her. How would she be able to look after herself and the baby without it?

It had been a shock when she found out that her mother, who for as long as she could remember had worked as a waitress at the largest hotel restaurant in Mariehamn, the Arkipelag, had amassed a fortune during her life.

A mystery man had been paying thousands of Euros each month into her savings account. The apartment that they shared until her mother had been moved to a nursing home was owned by her, rather than rented from the council as Frida had always believed. If only she'd discussed all of this with her mother before the dementia got so bad that she couldn't even recognize Frida, even though she visited her every day in the care home.

Frida had later found out that the man's name was Alexander Dudnikov, and that his dealings on the island had been investigated by Alicia when she worked for the local paper. He'd been convicted of money laundering in Sweden. Her lawyer told her that there was no evidence that the money she had inherited came from him.

But Frida isn't stupid.

At the time, when she'd been privy to this shocking detail, Frida was a new mother, with a baby to look after, and grieving for her own mom. The money had been more than welcome, removing the need to get a job and find a permanent childcare solution for Anne Sofie. She'd sold her mother's small flat on the outskirts of Mariehamn and bought the lovely three-bedroom apartment in the center of town, converted from an old shipowner's mansion into three luxury apartments.

How would she manage if she had to give up her home, and live without the monthly payments from her investments, which Karlsson, her and her mother's lawyer, had so carefully arranged for her?

Frida looks over to the market square opposite. There are a few older children on their skateboards using the empty space to practice their tricks. Frida watches them and thinks soon this will be Anne Sofie. She smiles, watching a girl with two long braids performing a sideways flip (is that what it's called?) in front of her. She wants to clap but her smile freezes when she remembers that if she – or Andrei – reports what she now knows about Dudnikov's (her father's!) activities, she will be financially ruined. She may not be able to afford even a skateboard for her daughter.

Frida puts her head in her hands and thinks. She has no education apart from her Baccalaureate, which she managed to scrape through while her mother was in the home.

She's had two jobs, one in the library when she was still at school and one at the local paper as an intern, but she didn't return after she had the baby. There was no need because of all the money.

She hasn't even thought about working again and has left any decision until Anne Sofie is older. Perhaps when she begins school, Frida had thought, she could do some voluntary work, or even set up her own charitable organization. She's always imagined doing some good with the money.

But what if she didn't have it?

Frida glances at her watch and realizes it is now twelve noon. She's late picking up Anne Sofie, so she gets up and rushes toward the nursery on the Esplanade.

Walking home with Anne Sofie in her stroller, Frida makes a decision. She will tell Andrei everything. About the article, which she doubts he's seen, especially since he doesn't speak Swedish.

She will also tell him who her father, and Anne Sofie's grandfather is. He has a right to know she suspects her father of being one of the Russians that brought Daniel to the islands. Whether it was people trafficking, the article didn't conclusively say, but it was heavily hinted at.

She knows Andrei will not want to have anything to do with her after she's told him everything. She also knows that he will not approve of her decision to keep the money.

If the tables were turned, there is no way she'd forgive him for something like that.

CHAPTER SIXTY-TWO

A licia finds Patrick outside the police station. There is no sign of the Romanian.

'I'll give you a lift back to Sjoland,' Alicia says, not looking at him.

During the drive back to the farm, Alicia and Patrick are silent. When she turns into the drive, she notices there's a third car in the small area in front of Hilda's yard. It's a rental, so it's most likely one that Leo has hired for his journey to the ferry port. Although that doesn't make much sense, because Hilda promised to drive him, but Alicia hasn't got time to think about it now.

She cuts the engine and sits with her head bent and her hands in her lap.

'You do know that you have to give the diary to Andrei?'

'I already have.'

Patrick sounds triumphant.

Alicia lifts her head and looks at his face. He's

grinning at her. She doesn't respond to his smile but keeps her mouth straight and looks down toward her lap.

'I still can't believe that Lars and the woman, Disa, your accountant, was behind it all!' Patrick says.

'You gave the diary to Andrei, when?'

'Outside the police station.'

Alicia nods.

At least Patrick has done something right. She lifts her eyes. 'I can't believe you took it!'

Patrick's face falls.

'I don't know what came over me. I was looking through it, and then I just put it inside my satchel. I'd completely forgotten about it when ...'

'When you decided to put your career before everything?'

Once again, Patrick has betrayed her. To think that he was holding onto a piece of evidence from a year back and hadn't told her. And then, to keep that evidence, which who knows, could have thrown a completely different light on poor Daniel's death, to himself without even telling her!

They'd been working together on the article and the case after all. Although their relationship had been particularly tumultuous at the time, with her still trying to deny her own feelings for him, he should have told her.

But she doesn't say any of this to Patrick. She doesn't want him to believe that she wants any kind of reconciliation. She places her forehead on the steering wheel and exhales deeply. She has to remain calm.

'Darling Alicia, I know I have made a mistake. Believe me when I say ...'

Patrick stops speaking.

'What's the matter?'

He places a hand on Alicia's shoulders, but she shrugs it off and lifts her head.

'I don't want to talk about it. The most important thing is that the diary is where it belongs.'

Alicia speaks slowly, controlling her voice, but not looking at him.

CHAPTER SIXTY-THREE

There is a silence in the car.

Patrick looks at Alicia. Her gaze is down and Patrick realizes he has no idea what's on her mind.

'Can you believe it?'

Patrick speaks softly. What they have found out that day must have come as a shock to Alicia. That's why she is so quiet.

'I know these things happen, but to a little farm in Åland, no,' Alicia replies slowly.

She's still not looking at Patrick.

'I feel sorry for Old Ledin,' Alicia adds and sighs.

'You sure he didn't know?'

Alicia lifts her eyes at Patrick. Her expression is serious.

'Absolutely.'

'And Disa, did you have any inkling?'

Alicia turns her face and looks out of the window toward the main house.

Patrick sees the sun is behind a thick cloud and it looks as if it might rain.

Alicia shakes her head.

'Who would have thought that a small-town book-keeper would be capable of such fraudulent behavior. But you never know about people, I guess,' Patrick says and puts his hand on Alicia's, which are resting on her lap.

'Is this for another story you are writing? Are you interviewing me again?'

Alicia's hostile tone surprises Patrick. He knows she's upset about the diary, but he's now done the right thing. He's also given up his job in Stockholm and helped her uncover the culprits on the farm. Surely, she should be happy about all of that?

Alicia glares at Patrick's hands. He quickly removes them. She faces Patrick, and the eyes now trained on him are dark, as dark as the clouds above them.

Perhaps it's a storm that's brewing, not just rain.

'No, of course not. I told you, I resigned.'

Patrick cannot understand what more Alicia wants him to do. He made a mistake, but it cannot be undone. He published a second story, making it clear his sources were unreliable. He's seen the article online already, although he wouldn't be surprised if Axelsson pulls it as soon as he realizes what Patrick has done. But he knows that once an article is out there, it can never be completely deleted.

'What are you going to do now?' Patrick asks.

He hesitates, and then touches Alicia's cheek. Perhaps she's just confused, taking her anger toward

Lars and Disa out on him. It's completely understandable.

'I think what you should do now ...'

Patrick starts speaking but Alicia interrupts him. Her actions are swift. She twists her head sideways, so that his hand drops.

'I think what I'm going to do next has nothing to do with you. And I think you should leave.'

With those words, Alicia leans over Patrick and opens his door.

'Now.'

At that moment, there is a loud crash and large droplets start falling from the sky. Patrick gazes at Alicia.

'But ...'

'Go!'

'Please, Alicia, I can ...'

Patrick doesn't finish his sentence. He sees in Alicia's expression a determination he hasn't noticed before. He gets out of the car and pulls the collar of his shirt up. But the heavy drops drench him, so he starts running toward his car.

CHAPTER SIXTY-FOUR

After the door to the Volvo has slammed shut, Alicia starts shivering. Rain is falling hard on the windshield and she puts her arms around herself.

Don't cry. He's not worth it.

She sees from the rear window Patrick run to his vehicle, start the engine, and turn onto the main road. She wonders briefly if he got very wet, but then discards the thought. She couldn't stand the sight of him and his touch for a moment longer.

How, she wonders to herself had she been duped by him for so long? She'd been planning a life with him, but at every turn, she now realizes, it had been entirely on his terms.

When he moved to Stockholm and asked her to come with him, it was so that he could pursue his own career at *Journalen*. Yet, he hadn't told her that the beautiful apartment overlooking the Riddarfjärden water, which they shared, was owned by his former in-laws. He'd used that apartment to woo Alicia into joining him in Stock-holm. She had to find out the truth from Mia, his ex.

The ex whom he slept with while Alicia was at home in Sjoland, looking after her mom after the sudden death of Uffe. And then, to cap it all, he turned up at the funeral, having been more of less absent during that painful period in her life, with – of all people – Mia! And he put it all down to the need for friendly relations for the sake of his daughters.

And I fell for it all.

How long, Alicia now wonders, would she have been blinded by him had Patrick not written the article?

When the lights from Patrick's car have disappeared from view, Alicia gets up and runs inside Hilda's house. She needs to fill her mom in on all that she has learned that day. The sooner she does this, the better.

When she opens the door, she hears voices from the kitchen. She throws her cardigan over the banister and steps inside.

At the kitchen table, three people are talking and drinking coffee. There's Hilda, sitting with her back to Alicia. She's pouring coffee into the cups. Opposite her sits Leo, and next to Hilda is another man. Alicia imme-diately recognizes the shape of his head, the light brown curly hair, the square shoulders, and his tall frame.

'What are you doing here?'

Liam turns and smiles.

'That's a nice welcome!'

The corners of Alicia's mouth lift up and she steps forward to greet him.

Liam rises from the table and envelops Alicia in a

hug. Being inside his arms, so familiar, makes Alicia relax. She takes in his scent and closes her eyes for a moment. But she cannot fall back into her old life, which Liam is part of, so she forces herself to move away from his embrace.

'It's good to see you,' Alicia says.

Liam's eyes are fixed on Alicia and she has to look away. The first time they met, when a migraine was hovering around her temples, she was mesmerized by those eyes. They were kind, yet interesting and even a little dangerous, and she couldn't refuse his invitation to a ball for the participants of a medical conference he was attending at her university.

It seems a million years ago now, but she still remembers how she'd fallen in love with Liam that same night. Or even as soon as he'd looked at her and spoken. He still has that soft, very faint, Irish accent, which Alicia could listen to all night.

But so much has happened to them since. The loss of their son, his unfaithfulness, her desire to move back home to the islands. Åland, which he didn't love in the same way as she did. His work as a surgeon always came first in their marriage, so there was never any chance he would give up London and join Alicia in Sjoland. Alicia isn't sure she ever wanted him to do that, either. Especially not after she'd met Patrick.

She too had broken the marriage vows.

CHAPTER SIXTY-FIVE

'Have you eaten?'

Hilda's words bring Alicia back to the present.

'No, and I'm starving, actually!'

Alicia laughs, for once her mom's constant catering is hitting the mark.

'Oh, in that case! We had salmon chowder, would you like some? It seems perfect for this weather.'

Hilda gets up and goes over to the stove. There's an enamel pot of delicious-smelling soup standing over one of the gas rings. She takes a bowl and begins to ladle chowder into it.

'We've already eaten, but there's plenty left over. I've also got rhubarb pie for dessert which we were just about to start, but we can wait for you.'

Gazing at the pot, Alicia feels famished. When did she last have something to eat?

'That's sounds lovely, but you don't have to wait for me. We're all family here, after all.

Alicia sits next to her real father and grins at him.

'You've had salmon and milk?' She whispers so that her mom can't hear.

Leo nods and shrugs. But on his face is a wide smile and his eyes are sparkling.

'Your mother wouldn't let me leave until we know how you got on,' Leo replies out loud.

Hilda comes over to the table, placing the bowl of soup in front of Alicia and a basket of rye bread next to it.

'Eat!'

For a moment everyone is silent while Alicia takes a spoonful of chowder.

'It's delicious, Mom!'

Hilda smiles at Alicia and glances at Liam.

'How did you get on? And where's Patrick?'

She knows, as well as Alicia, how much the two men hate each other.

Alicia ignores Hilda's question about Patrick but, between mouthfuls of chowder, gives a brief summary of what she found out.

Halfway through, she turns to Liam and mouths, 'Sorry' in English.

'Don't worry,' he says, bringing his palms up.

'So, both you, Mom, Uffe, and me, it seems, have been fooled into thinking we were getting a good deal for the farm with the Eastern European labor. But all along, Lars and Disa were skimming off a payment for themselves. Both have now disappeared, but Ebba has put out a search warrant for them. I don't for one moment think they'll ever be found, but one can but hope.'

'What about the poor boys?' Hilda asks.

Her eyes are wide, and her mouth has remained open all the while Alicia has been recounting the sorry tale.

'It looks like they were severely taken advantage of. It could even be classed as modern slavery. Ebba will pursue the matter from now on. There might be a court case – eventually.'

Hilda puts a hand over her mouth.

'Oh my God!'

Alicia places her palm over her mom's other arm, resting on the table.

'Uffe didn't know anything about the whole thing. I don't think he even suspected, but I really don't know.'

'That's right, Hilda. I'm sure your Uffe is innocent in all of this.'

Leo leans over the table, taking hold of Hilda's hands.

'I'm certain he was a fine man. As such, he would have refused to have anything to do with this if he knew,' he says softly to Hilda.

They're suddenly getting on well, Alicia thinks.

Hilda rises from the table and goes to stand by the kitchen counter. Alicia follows her and gives her shoulders a squeeze with one arm. They stand there, with their backs to the two men.

'It's OK, Mom. Nobody thinks any of us knew about all of this.'

Hilda is still, looking out of the small window over

the sea. There are high, white-topped waves on the water, and rain is lashing the windows.

'Look at this weather,' Hilda sighs.

Alicia notices that tears are running down her mom's face and she turns to give her a hug.

'I miss him too,' she whispers into her mom's ear and Hilda nods, placing her head on Alicia's shoulder. Her body slumps and Alicia has to squeeze tighter to keep them both upright.

Alicia is taken aback by this simple act, so unlike Hilda, who always wants to appear strong toward Alicia. Even when crying for Uffe over the months since his sudden passing, she has been dignified in her grief.

After Alicia decided to stay on and take over the running of the farm, Hilda was full of plans for how they were going to modernize Uffe's barn, so that Alicia would be comfortable living and working there.

At the same time, she began a business of her own. Sadly, her B&B venture hasn't yet taken off. In spite of all this, she took on Leo's visit, with vigour and energy. Something Alicia now sees she should not have asked her mom to do.

And now, it seems as if all the fight has gone out of her mother.

'It's OK, just let it all go,' Alicia says softly.

Suddenly Hilda straightens her back and smiles through her tears. 'Goodness, look at me, a cry baby!'

Turning to the kitchen table and the men sitting there, looking uncomfortable, she continues, 'Liam, Leo, I am sorry. Please eat.'

She waves her hand, indicating the delicious-looking

rhubarb pie. There's also a small bowl of whipped cream. Liam shifts on his seat and glances at Alicia. If possible, he looks even more awkward than Leo.

'Can you tell your husband to take some pie?' Hilda says to Alicia.

Alicia smiles. And so, in a nanosecond, her mom is back.

CHAPTER SIXTY-SIX

That evening, Andrei and Frida are sitting side by side on her mother's old sofa. At the table in front of them is Daniel's diary, which Andrei has read twice now. He's translated some bits, mainly those that mention Frida, to her.

'Your brother was lovely,' Frida says.

Andrei straightens his back and Frida sees there's pride in his face when he replies, 'Yes, he is.'

Frida fights the tears when she hears Andrei's words. She knows that using the present tense is most probably an error and due to his not-so-perfect English but talking of Daniel as if he was still here is just too much for her. To calm down, and get the courage to say what she has to, she takes in a lungful of air and blows it out of her mouth.

'Look, I have to tell you something.'

Andrei's eyebrows knit together.

'What?'

'My father is Russian.'

Frida is surprised by Andrei's reaction.

A wide smile lights up his face. He places an arm over Frida's shoulders and pulls her to himself.

'I do not hate all Russians!'

Frida frees herself from his embrace and continues, 'No, you don't understand. My father's name is Alexander Dudnikov and he was here. He is a criminal. He gave all this money to my mother and she left it to me. But I don't know where it came from.'

As if to indicate her riches, Frida sweeps her hand over the living room and the view across the stormy sea beyond.

'I do not understand.'

'He is a nasty man. He has been charged with money laundering and suspected of people trafficking. He may have been involved in how Daniel came here.'

Now Andrei is staring at Frida.

Frida takes hold of his hands and continues to speak quickly.

'But I don't have any evidence and neither have the police. And Daniel had an accident at sea, I'm certain of that. I would have told you if I thought anything else.'

Andrei gets up and lets Frida's hands drop. He goes over to the window, looking at the rain which is now almost obscuring the view of the sea. You can just make out the rocking masts of the large schooner *Pommern* in the distance, but the shoreline opposite the West Harbor is shrouded by mist and fog.

Frida doesn't know what to do.

. . .

Watching the rain beating down the windows and the large sailing ship in the distance, Andrei is thinking hard and fast.

Dudnikov.

Has he heard that name before?

He shakes his head. No, he doesn't think so. Daniel never mentioned the name either to him before he left, or in his letters or diary.

He turns around to look at Frida, who's sitting on the sofa, gazing up at him and wringing her hands.

Can he trust her? Is she speaking the truth?

'But I know Daniel can fish and be in boat at sea!'

Frida jumps up at his words and comes to stand next to him.

'But you don't! He wasn't that good, honestly. He wanted to think he was, but with the cast on his foot, which made him very clumsy, he could quite easily have capsized. And believe me, Ebba, the police chief, did investigate thoroughly. I know she did. It was Alicia who wanted it to be Dudnikov. He'd been intimidating her mom, Hilda, you see ... She – we – didn't know at the time that he was my father.'

'I don't understand,' Andrei says.

'Look, come and sit down and I will tell you everything.'

Andrei lets himself be led back to the sofa. He listens carefully while Frida tells him how Dudnikov loaned some money to Hilda and how he frightened her after she couldn't pay the large sum he began to demand. And how Ebba had investigated him, but he had fled back to

Russia before she could question him. And how no one has heard from him since.

'He could even be dead, for all I know. Or care.'

'But the money?'

Andrei's face reveals nothing.

Frida puts a strand of her hair in her mouth and takes it out again.

'My attorney says that no one knows where my mother got all the money from. There is no trace of the benefactor – the person who paid large sums into her account over the years. So, I've kept it. For Anne Sofie's sake.'

Once she's finished talking, she lowers her head. She can't look at Andrei because she knows what she will see there.

She waits for him to tell her that he will leave. Perhaps he would have left her anyway? How can she compete with his farm and the responsibility he has to his two siblings. Perhaps it's for the best that he goes sooner rather than later.

When Andrei doesn't say anything, Frida speaks again. She can't look at him, but she has to tell him what she has decided.

'I've made an appointment to see my lawyer. I have a plan for what to do with the money.'

She recounts her ideas and when she's finished, slowly lifts her eyes up to Andrei.

He's gazing at her, his eyes wide.

'Why you do this?'

'To make things right.'

'But you can't!'

'Watch me,' Frida says.

They stare at each other for a moment, before Frida decides to make a move. She pushes her face close to Andrei and presses her lips against his.

To her relief, Andrei responds to her kiss. He takes her into his arms. Andrei pulls his face away from Frida's for a moment and says, 'You incredible woman.'

CHAPTER SIXTY-SEVEN

Parking her car outside Marie Bar in Mariehamn, Alicia glances at her watch and sees she's going to be late. It's still raining heavily as she walks briskly along Köpmannagatan, dodging tourists, who are meandering slowly along the sidewalks with all the time in the world, even in the rain.

She is puzzled why Frida would want her to join her meeting with Karlsson. She's managed her affairs on her own so far, hardly even asking for advice.

Why now?

Alicia absolutely approves of giving some of the money to good causes. It's what she would have done too, but surely Frida could have done all of this on her own?

While she's hurrying along the street, she also thinks about Liam and how happy having him on the islands makes her.

For the first time in years, since she's been back living in her childhood home, she feels like her old self.

Almost as content as she was when she came here and spent two weeks with Stefan. Of course, his loss will never leave her and sadness about her wonderful son is still a constant presence, but she is stronger.

At last, she arrives at the lawyer's office. Frida is already there, looking nervous.

The two women hug each other.

'Where's little Anne Sofie?' Alicia asks and realizes immediately that it sounded like an accusation.

Frida raises her eyebrows but keeps her voice level.

'I left her with Andrei.'

'Oh.'

Alicia cannot hide her surprise. Does Frida know the man well enough for baby-sitting?

'He is her uncle, after all.'

Now Alicia is stunned.

'You told him!'

Frida looks at Alicia but doesn't reply.

'I'm sorry, Frida, I don't know what's up with me. That's great. I presume he was delighted?'

The girl nods.

At that moment, the door opens and Frida's lawyer, whom Alicia has only met in passing before, opens the door to his office.

CHAPTER SIXTY-EIGHT

The smell of the lawyer's aftershave gives Frida a horrible flashback to the first time she'd visited Mr Karlsson's office, just days after her mother had passed away. Sorrow and longing for her mom hits Frida so hard that she has to take several deep breaths. Her mother has been gone for over a year now, but grief can still suddenly grab her, reminding her how alone she's felt since losing her.

'Miss Anttila, what a lovely surprise. And Miss Ulsson!'

Karlsson's mouth is pulled into a fake smile as he gets up from behind his vast, dark wooden desk and comes around to take first Frida's then Alicia's hand.

Frida manages to calm her breathing and gives Alicia a sideways smile. None of the islanders are capable of grasping the fact that Alicia has been married for more than twenty years to Liam and is now called Mrs O'Connell. But then, Frida thinks, maybe Alicia prefers to be known by her maiden name.

'Alicia, please,' Alicia says, seemingly unconcerned about the lawyer's misstep.

Karlsson walks around and returns to his desk.

'Please take a seat,' he says and adds, 'What can I do for you two lovely ladies?'

The lawyer grins widely and places his hands on his desk, pulling his chair closer to the edge.

Alicia gives Frida an encouraging nod.

'I'd like to spend some of my money.'

'OK.'

'I would like to give a large sum to the Tamas family in Romania.'

This makes the old lawyer's eyes widen. He takes off his thin-rimmed glasses and peers at Frida. His eyes without his spectacles look bare and he seems almost vulnerable.

Alicia, too, turns toward Frida.

'Are you sure?'

Frida ignores both the lawyer and Alicia's reaction.

'Andrei Tamas is Anne Sofie's uncle and I want to give him 250 thousand Euros.'

'What?' the lawyer and Alicia say in unison.

Frida turns to Alicia and says, 'I know what I am doing.'

Alicia sighs.

The lawyer starts to say something but Frida interrupts him and continues speaking.

'He runs the family farm in southern Romania, and I want to open an account for him, where he can draw it out whenever he wishes.'

'He will have to pay tax on such a large sum,' the lawyer says after a moment.

'In that case, please advise me how I can do this to minimize costs for both of us.'

Karlsson nods a few times.

'I need a little time, but if you are certain. Perhaps an annuity of some kind?'

'Ok,' Frida says and adds, 'With the rest of the money, I wish to start a charity.'

'Well, that's not so easy,' he states.

'Why not?' Frida demands.

Karlsson leans back in his chair.

'Because first of all, you need to know what cause you want to support. Next, you need to appoint a board, apply for the National Charity Register, and so on. It's quite complicated.'

'But you can help, isn't that right?' Alicia says, raising her eyebrows and glancing at Frida. She seems to have got over the shock of Frida's decision to support Andrei.

'Yes, of course.'

The lawyer is concentrating on cleaning his glasses.

'How much of your funds would you like to use to set up this charity?'

'All of it,' Frida replies immediately.

'Well, I'm not sure I'd advise that!'

'But it's up to me, isn't it?'

Slowly, oh so slowly, Karlsson replaces his glasses on his nose and places his hands on top of each other on his desk.

'Yes, of course. What cause did you have in mind? You do know that there are several good campaigns you could support instead of setting up something of your own, which is always a much more costly venture. There is also the time you need to devote to the administration and so on ...'

Frida has had enough.

'Look, Mr Karlsson. I know my real father may have come by all this money in some illegal way, so I want to use it to negate his actions.'

Karlsson coughs. Again, he takes a long time to reply, as if approaching each and every word with utmost caution. He leans toward Frida.

With his eyes firmly fixed on her face, the lawyer says, 'Now, you know full well that I have no information on this. I have never met the person who placed all the money in your mother's bank account over the years. Everything is fully within the legal framework. I can assure you that it's absolutely above board. You do not need to worry about any of this.'

Frida stares at the lawyer. She's incapable of playing these games.

'I know that you are aware that my father is Alexander Dudnikov and that he is most likely behind the people trafficking that *Journalen* reported in its paper on Sunday. I have had a visit from Daniel's brother, who has letters and a diary in his possession. Daniel mentioned two Russians who organized his travel to Scandinavia, and who seemed to control all aspects of his life. Although my father's name isn't mentioned in the article, nor in any of the letters Daniel sent to his brother, all of the hallmarks are there.'

Karlsson is visibly shocked.

'I did see the article, but didn't the journalist, Kurt Eriksson's son-in-law, refute the allegations? And you have never been involved in this, have you? No one has come to you with any kinds of accusations?'

Frida is hanging her head now.

'No. But can't you see, I must do something.'

The lawyer is quiet. After a while, he says, 'You are a wealthy woman, Miss Anttila. Why are you concerned about a man who has never been your father? Has never, as far as I know, even met you? But, he did something that many fathers do not, and has provided handsomely for you without wanting anything in return. As far as I can see, you are in a very fortunate position indeed.'

Karlsson straightens his back and adds, 'Go home and think about this. Let the idea develop. If, in a week or two, you still wish to go ahead, come back and see me. Now, if you two ladies would excuse me, I am a very busy man, so ...' he stretches out his arm, and with the open palm of his right hand indicates for Frida and Alicia to leave.

But Frida is not about to be fobbed off with platitudes.

'If you can't help me, there are other lawyers who can. I want to set up a charity to stop human trafficking to the Nordic countries. Not just to the islands, but all of Scandinavia.' Frida takes Alicia's hand.

'And I have my first trustee right here.'

Karlsson sighs.

For a moment, he gazes at Frida, and Alicia, his expression almost pitying.

'Alright. But at least consider saving some funds for a rainy day?'

Frida turns to look at Alicia before replying. The older woman nods.

'OK, agreed.'

Karlsson gets up and stretches his hand toward the two women.

'I will be in touch to let you know the process and what needs to happen when. There will be some costs on my part too, you understand.'

Frida takes the lawyer's hand.

'Yes, of course.'

'Now, I do have another appointment. It was good to see you Miss Anttila and Miss Ulsson.'

CHAPTER SIXTY-NINE

The first sound Frida hears when she returns home is Anne Sofie's giggling. Andrei is on the floor on all fours while the little girl crawls underneath him. The kitten sits between Andrei's shoulders watching the baby. Each time Anne Sofie emerges from underneath Andrei's body and he looks back at her, she dissolves into hysterical laughter.

When she spots Frida, she stops and lifts up her arms. 'Mamma, mamma.'

Andrei scoops her up and brings the baby to Frida.

'You've been OK then?'

Andrei nods. He strokes Anne Sofie's wispy blonde hair.

'I'm going to miss this little one.'

Frida and Andrei's eyes meet.

'I spoke with my brother this morning.'

'OK.'

Frida can't hear any more. She puts Anne Sofie on

the high chair and gets a bottle of formula from the fridge.

'I'd better get her settled. It's time for her nap,' she says as she waits for the milk to warm.

Suddenly she feels Andrei's arms around her.

'Frida,' he whispers into her ear. 'I'm going home to organize everything, but I will return.'

He turns her around and looks deeply into her eyes. 'You believe me, don't you?'

Frida nods, trying to hold back the tears pricking her eyes. She doesn't know whether they are tears of joy at his words, or tears for the longing she knows she will have for him when he's gone.

'We call each other every day or all the time. I can show you my brother and sister and my cows.'

Frida cannot help but laugh.

'I'm really looking forward to meeting your cows.'

A squeal from the baby, who feels ignored, fills the air and they both turn toward Anne Sofie.

'Patience, my darling!' Frida says and goes to pick her up.

Andrei also comes over, to fold Frida and the little girl in an embrace.

'I love you,' he whispers into Frida's ear.

Frida feels as if her heart is about to explode with happiness.

'I love you too.'

CHAPTER SEVENTY

'Tell me what's been going on? You told me you'd been trying to sort out labor for the farm, and that Lars wanted to bring back boys from Romania. Your mom told me that Patrick had written this article. I read it, but I'm not sure I understood all of it.'

Alicia and Liam are sitting in Alicia's cottage, with glasses of red wine in front of them. Alicia is seated at one end of the corner sofa, while Liam is at the other. They are facing each other.

Alicia begins to recount the whole story, finishing with Andrei's visit and Frida's plans to give him some money and start up a charity.

'Wow, your mom did fill me in on some of it, but I didn't know about Frida and Andrei.'

A wave of tiredness washes over Alicia as the effects of the food she had at the main house, and the wine she's been sipping since they moved back to her cottage about half an hour ago, take hold.

Hilda and Leo have left for the ferry – Leo is finally returning home to Helsinki.

Alicia is still not quite clear what has happened between her parents, but Leo said before getting in Hilda's car that he is coming back 'soon'. Hilda didn't comment, so Alicia assumes that this next visit has been agreed between her parents.

Strange how a crisis brings people together as well as drives them apart.

She decides not to think any more about Patrick. He's history. Suddenly, she takes in what Liam has been saying.

'In what language did you talk to my mom? And had that article been translated into English? Already?'

Liam has a cheeky smile on his face.

'I've been learning Swedish.'

'What?'

'Men jag kan inte tala so bra ännu.'

Liam's Swedish pronunciation is very attractive, with that same, faint, Irish pitch to it.

Alicia puts her hand to her mouth. She's speechless. Liam, who's always claimed that he's rubbish at languages, has been learning Swedish!

Not once during their twenty-year marriage, when they visited the islands at least once a year, staying for two weeks at a time, had he felt the need to learn more than the very basic phrases of 'Yes', 'No', and 'Thank You'.

'I was a complete fool before, not even trying.'

Alicia is still staring at Liam. She cannot believe

what she is learning about her ex-husband. She leans toward Liam and places a hand on his arm.

'There was no need for you to learn Swedish before.'

'But you would have wanted me to. I know you would, and I'm so sorry I didn't. It would have made it easier for you to speak Swedish with Stefan.'

They are silenced by the mention of their late son. Alicia removes her hand from Liam's arm and takes a large gulp of her wine, finishing the drink.

'A top-up?' She asks, after noticing that Liam's glass, like hers, is empty.

'Yes, please. I'm staying with Hilda, so I don't have to drive into town.'

'That's your rental outside?'

Alicia moves toward the kitchen and Liam speaks to her back.

'Yeah. I thought it would be easier, and I wouldn't be reliant on you guys.'

As she pours more wine into the two glasses, Alicia wonders what the real reason for Liam's visit to the islands is.

'My Swedish isn't perfect, but my teacher says I'm making good progress. She tells me that time on the islands would be the best thing for my language development.'

Liam accepts the drink from Alicia and gazes up at her.

'I'm sure she's right.'

CHAPTER SEVENTY-ONE

A sudden ray of sunshine hits the wooden floor of the cottage and Alicia exclaims, 'Look, it's stopped raining!'

She goes and opens the double doors onto a large decking area. The wooden steps leading down to the jetty and the sea are glistening and the birdsong is almost deafening.

Alicia leans on the doorframe and thinks how much she loves this place.

The weather alone is a marvel. In summer, one moment the sky is the color of dark steel, and the next, the clouds are fluffy white balls and the sun is shining down in full force. In winter, the temperatures go so far below zero that you can sometimes ski on the frozen sea.

Now the wind is brisk and the waves are white-topped farther out to the Lumparn water.

'It's a wonderful view.'

Alicia turns around to smile at Liam, who's come to stand behind her.

She takes in his face, so open and soft. Gone is the pain that was etched onto his features for so long after they lost Stefan.

'How are you, really?' Liam asks.

His tone, which is tender, once again reminds Alicia of the day they met all those years ago.

She nods.

'Surprisingly, I am OK. I feel that Uffe is vindicated, and I also feel that the boys, including Daniel, will get justice. Ebba will see to it, I'm certain.'

'That's good.'

They both stand still for a moment, gazing out to sea. The wind is beginning to die down and suddenly Alicia spots an Arctic loon in the distance.

'Look!' She says, pointing out to sea. At that moment the bird dives into the water.

'Wait till you see it emerge. These divers go for metres under water.'

They wait by the door, standing still so as not to scare the bird, even though they are a little away from the water.

And there, after a few minutes, the diver emerges, first its long black beak, then its dark gray plumage. It shakes its wings, revealing its bright white breast feathers briefly, before settling down to a slow progress toward the shore.

'They're a protected species here.'

Alicia turns toward Liam. Suddenly she notices the familiar shape of his lips. She inhales the scent of soap and the citrus cologne he always wears. Her heart begins to beat faster, and she feels a tingling along her spine.

Liam takes Alicia's glass from her and places it, together with his own, on a small side table Alicia has placed in the corner next to the doors.

When Liam lifts her chin to kiss her, she is surprised at how good it feels. To begin with, he's gentle, touching his lips to hers, but soon, he becomes more insistent, and his tongue enters her mouth. Alicia responds and Liam presses her body closer to his. She removes herself from his embrace and takes a breath.

'Look Liam ...'

'You want it too. I can feel it.'

Liam is standing in front of her, and she can see his erection at the front of his jeans. She blows air out of her lungs.

How easy it would be to just take him to my bed now? It isn't as if we haven't done it thousands of times before. And as it is, we are still married, officially at least.

'I do, but ...'

Liam places his hand on Alicia's cheek.

'I'm sorry, I'm too impatient. I love you so much.'

His eyes are dark and full of lust, but Alicia can also see tenderness in them and in his gestures.

'How long are you staying?'

Liam takes one step away and turns toward the sea again.

'You do really love this place, don't you?'

Alicia nods and follows Liam's gaze out toward the jetty and the now calm waters beyond.

'I do.'

Liam takes a deep intake of breath and blows the air out again.

'Well, in that case, so do I. Or, at least, I will learn to love it for your sake.'

Alicia turns toward Liam and stares at him.

'What are you saying?'

'I have put in my notice at St John's. I'm now on holiday for two weeks and I will be leaving the hospital and my practice at the end of September. If you let me, I will move here and start practicing on the islands. I've looked into the conversion courses and the process isn't too arduous. With my savings and the money I'll get from the flat in town, I can survive without work – if need be – for a few months, even a year.'

Alicia's head is spinning, and she feels faint. She stumbles, and Liam takes hold of her elbow, guiding her back to the sofa.

'Lie down.'

He puts his fingers around Alicia's wrist and, looking at his watch, takes her pulse.

'A bit high, but that's to be expected.'

Liam's eyes are full of concern.

'I'm sorry. I didn't plan to tell you everything tonight, but I just couldn't wait,' he says.

'I....' Alicia begins, but Liam puts his finger gently on her lips.

'Don't say anything now. We can talk about this later. I don't want to stay in London. The new apartment is wonderful, but the lifestyle. The city, the hospital. It's too busy.'

Alicia closes her eyes. She can't think straight. Liam here, on the islands? Is he really willing to give up his hard-won position at the hospital in London?

Liam continues, 'I just can't take the stress anymore. But I won't move here if you don't want me to. I can find somewhere in the countryside, or even go back to Ireland.'

Liam stops talking.

Alicia opens her eyes.

'I don't know what to say.'

'You don't have to say anything. Let's just enjoy the evening together.'

Alicia smiles at Liam's words.

'Yes let's.'

She gets up and sits down next to Liam. Their knees are touching, and they sit like that for a moment, gazing at the peaceful sea view. Alicia glances sideways at Liam, while pushing her left knee against his.

'What are you going to do about the farm now?'

Liam's question is a valid one.

Alicia has been thinking hard.

'I managed to get old Jonsson for the harvest, starting tomorrow. He's bringing his grandson. He's only sixteen but apparently very keen on staying here in Åland and working the land.'

'There you are then. Lars was talking rubbish for his own ends.'

Alicia smiles at Liam, 'It appears so.

Liam perches on the sofa and moves himself closer to Alicia.

'I've been doing some research myself. And there is one thing you could do to try to increase your profit margins here.'

Alicia stares at Liam. He's never taken much interest in the farm, well, not when Uffe was still in charge.

'Oh, yeah?'

'You could set up a small operation manufacturing your own potato chips. I saw this clip on YouTube. It was part of a cookery program, actually.'

Alicia cannot but gaze at him. Liam has never been interested in how food is made, let alone a cookery program.

'Go on.'

She tries to sound encouraging and stop the smile that's hovering around her lips.

Liam looks at Alicia and grins.

'Not my usual TV watching, but anyway. The woman, I can't remember her name, went to visit this potato farm in East Anglia. They do exactly what you do, but, and here's the difference, they make their own gourmet chips. And presumably sell them directly to shops and restaurants. I can see that doing it this way would give you much more money, don't you think? The chip-making didn't seem complicated. You'd have to invest in the machinery, but you've certainly got enough room here, right? And Hilda could help you with it.'

Liam is talking with his hands, and suddenly gets up.

'You've got that empty barn where you park the cars

in winter, right? I can't see that it would take much to turn that into a potato chip factory!'

Alicia's thinking fast. Liam could have a point. She's often wondered why there isn't a more select brand of chips on the islands. Krisp used to be owned by the islanders, but it has long since been sold to an American corporation. This could be a new start for the islands as well as for the farm.

'What do you think?'

Liam is so excited that he looks as if he is about to take flight. He's rubbing his hands together and changing his weight from one foot to another.

'That could work,' Alicia says carefully.

'Yes! I knew you'd love the idea.'

Liam comes back to the sofa and leans toward Alicia. 'I want to sell my new apartment. It'll be worth a pretty penny. If I buy something here in Mariehamn, say a small studio or one-bedroom apartment, there'll be plenty left over to invest in this venture.'

Now Alicia is even more amazed.

'You'd do that?'

'Yes, it's my idea. A family business.'

'We could ask Frida too, and I have my share of the sale of the house in Crouch End.'

Liam looks a little deflated, but Alicia continues, 'It would be good to spread the risk, wouldn't it? Frida is looking to do some good with her money, and I'm sure securing the farm's future would serve that purpose. Wouldn't it be lovely if Anne Sofie was part of the future of the farm? The place where her father was at his happiest?'

Now Alicia feels a little tearful.

Liam sees the change in her face and takes hold of her shoulders.

'That's a nice thought.'

They hug for a long time, each thinking of the past as well as of the future. Even though Frida's little girl isn't their granddaughter, Alicia feels as if she is related to both Frida and Anne Sofie. With what Liam just said, he must feel the same.

'What about a swim?' Alicia says.

CHAPTER SEVENTY-TWO

L iam is amazed at how refreshing swimming in the sea is. Why had he always refused a dip on previous visits to the island?

Seeing Alicia revel in the chilly water in itself is a pleasure. His own skin protests violently as he puts his toes in. He has to muffle a yelp when he reaches the bottom of the small ladder at the end of the jetty.

All he wants to do is to get back up and run inside the house. He resists the temptation and slowly, urged by Alicia's shouts of 'Come on Liam!', lowers his whole body into the chilly Baltic.

Once he's totally immersed in the sea, and he's given himself a few moments to adjust, while wildly moving his arms and legs under the water, the sensation in his body is indescribably invigorating. The water caresses his joints in a wonderful way, and he doesn't want to get out.

But Alicia insists, 'We will catch a chill.'

Liam almost laughs at her words.

When he's out of the water again, standing on the jetty, wrapped in a large towel, he is grinning at his ex-wife like a teenage boy.

'That was wonderful!'

He moves toward Alicia and wraps her inside his arms and the sheet. He lifts her up and together they jump up and down. Alicia giggles like a little girl and Liam cannot stop himself. He goes down to kiss her lips, which are looking a little blue, something which stops him just in time.

'We need to go inside. You're cold.'

Back in the cottage, when Alicia has lit a wooden stove on the back wall of the living space, she offers Liam a whiskey.

'For the circulation,' she says and grins.

Liam has changed back to his clothes, but the sensation that he has somehow been purified by the dip in the sea remains.

'You should try that after a good sauna,' Alicia says with a glint in her eyes.

'I shall.'

Liam lifts his glass and gazes at Alicia with a wide smile.

'I can't promise I will love it, but I will try.'

CHAPTER SEVENTY-THREE

H aving Liam in her cottage, reading on her sofa, seems the most natural of things. Yet, it's far from that. Over the twenty or so years of their marriage, her husband never seemed to fit in on their visits to the islands, let alone enjoy his break away from London. He was tense, constantly on guard against some unusual – or unpleasant – food or tradition he was going to be subjected to.

He hated the sauna, something Hilda and Alicia often teased him about. But Alicia knew that he didn't enjoy the jokes. He really didn't enjoy the fishing trips Uffe took him on either, or the berry picking in the forest that Alicia insisted he should do with Stefan.

Why had she been so unforgiving?

Now Liam is sitting next to her on the sofa, sipping his Irish whiskey after their bracing swim in the Baltic.

'I can't believe you actually swam. I saw from the temperature gauge that the water was only 18°C.'

'Yeah, I saw that too. But I feel wonderful now.'

Liam smiles at Alicia and brings his half-full tumbler toward her. They clink glasses and take another sip.

'Besides, if it means I get to taste some of your stash of whiskey, I'm happy.'

Liam's grin widens and Alicia is reminded of Liam as a young man. His hair has thinned slightly, and a few lines have formed on his forehead, making him look even more intelligent.

It was his brains, but also his kindness, that had attracted Alicia to Liam. The way he was late for their first date because his colleague was critically ill, after which he had to fight his way through a snowstorm to find her student apartment, proved to Alicia that she was right in her first assessment of him.

When she fell pregnant and they became parents so very soon after marriage, Liam was the perfect father, even though his work schedule as a trainee surgeon was punishing.

'You were a good dad.'

Alicia's words seem to startle Liam. He raises his eyebrows and looks at her.

'Thank you.'

They are both silent for a moment, deep in thought.

'I am sorry I let him have the bike,' Liam says eventually.

Alicia stares at her husband. Has he been blaming himself all along? Did she think he was responsible for the accident too? Perhaps in the early days ...

'Stefan's death wasn't your fault.'

'I think it was. If I hadn't first let him borrow Uffe's

moped here, and then got him the bike in London, he would never have ...'

Alicia moves closer to Liam and, placing her glass on the low coffee table in front of them, puts a hand on his thigh.

'Listen, something else would have gone wrong. We can't turn the clock back. What happened, happened. Of course, I'd give anything for him still to be with us, but Stefan was a strong-headed boy. He always knew what he wanted and usually got it. Right?'

Alicia gazes up at Liam's face. She can see that his eyes are moist and he's biting his lower lip. He's hanging his head.

'Please don't, you'll get me going,' she adds, speaking softly.

'Sorry.'

Liam's voice is trembling, and Alicia cannot stand it any longer. She puts both of her arms around Liam and hugs him hard.

'Shh, it's OK. Let's cry together.'

Alicia rocks Liam as if he was a baby, and hears faint sobs. Strangely, Alicia's tears don't come. Perhaps she's already cried too much, and she has none left. She just holds onto Liam's manly, strong body.

It feels good to be able to comfort him. A sudden thought occurs to her: she's never consoled him in this way. It was always Liam who looked after her. Whether it was a medical issue, or emotional needs. She was the one who needed help.

Even when Liam was so seasick during the ferry journeys to the islands, he never asked for help, or accepted it. So, she let him be. But surely, she should have been more insistent? Especially after they lost Stefan.

Alicia lets go of Liam but continues to rub his back. She grabs a tissue box at the side of the sofa and hands it to Liam.

'Thank you,' he says, blowing his nose loudly. 'Sorry,' he adds.

'No need to be. Look, can we start afresh? I have so much going on with the farm, and Leo, my dad, and Mom, but if you are serious about making a go of it here on the islands ...'

'I am!' Liam interrupts her and takes hold of Alicia's hands.

'I want that more than anything. I know it won't be easy, but I am fed up with being alone. I love you and want to be close to you, even if we're not, you know, physically close.'

'Let's see about that.'

Alicia grins.

'That swim was impressive, so if you keep that up, you never know what will happen next.'

Liam manages a small smile.

'I knew that was a test.'

Alicia feigns shock.

'No, it wasn't!'

She thumps Liam with one of the small cushions scattered on the sofa. They both laugh, but suddenly Liam becomes serious and gazes at her intently. He opens his mouth as if to say something, but then closes it again.

'What, what is it?' Alicia asks.

'I know it's not my place to ask, but you and Patrick. Is it over?'

Alicia nods.

'Yes, that is most definitely over. But I can't hop from one man to another. I need some time to recoup and to think. You understand that, don't you?'

It's Liam's turn to nod his head. His lips turn up into a smile, when he replies, 'Fine by me. I'll wait as long as it takes.'

THE DAY WE MET

Don't forget your free story!

The Day We Met is set at Uppsala University in Sweden where Alicia is studying English. When a migraine is threatening to ruin her day, the last thing she expects is to meet the man of her dreams.

Liam, a British doctor, is in Uppsala attending a medical conference when a tall blonde chooses to sit at the same table as him in the busy student canteen. There's something beguiling about the young woman.

Go to helenahalme.com to sign up to my Readers' Group and get your free story now!

FROM THE AUTHOR

Dear Reader,

I hope you enjoyed *An Island Summer*!

To be completely honest with you, I wasn't planning to write another story in the *Love on the Island* series set on the Åland Islands, but the characters keep pulling me in with their complicated lives. So much so that I have already started writing Book 5 (yet untitled)!

An Island Summer is the second book I've written in a Covid lockdown. Although I love daydreaming about my beloved islands, it was far more difficult to transport myself there this time around. I am hoping against hope that I will be able to visit later this year, but who knows what will happen in the future. I have learned to be patient …

As always, my support team has kept my spirits up and enabled me to write and complete *An Island Summer*. Firstly, my ever patient and wise Englishman, David, and my family – Markus, Rebecca, Monika and little Alice. Without you, I would not be able to do what I do.

A further pillar of strength is my Big Sis, Anne. Our daily hour-long telephone conversations have given me laughter and tears in equal measure and reminded me of my (very strong) Finnish roots. Again, I very much hope I may be able to see her this summer on the islands.

My Readers' Group and my Launch Team must also be mentioned. I am buoyed by your many replies to my weekly emails. I've come to think of you as an expanded group of friends. During the many lockdowns of the past year, you have given me hope and spurred me on to write. Those of you who also took the time to read and comment on the Advance Reader copy of *An Island Summer* are true stars. Thank you!

Last but not least, thanks must go to my editor, Dorothy Stannard. Her professionalism and accuracy enable me to develop the stories and keep my characters true from one book to the next.

I have taken some liberties with place names on Åland. All the characters and plot lines are entirely made up. If they bear any resemblance to reality, this is purely coincidental.

Keep safe and well,

Helena Halme

London May 2021

ALSO BY HELENA HALME

The Nordic Heart Series:

The Young Heart (Prequel)

The English Heart (Book 1)

The Faithful Heart (Book 2)

The Good Heart (Book 3)

The True Heart (Book 4)

The Christmas Heart (Book 5)

The Nordic Heart Boxset Books 1-4

Love on the Island Series:

The Day We Met: Prequel Short Story

The Island Affair (Book 1)

An Island Christmas (Book 2)

The Island Daughter (Book 3)

An Island Summer (Book 4)

Other novels:

Coffee and Vodka: A Nordic family drama

The Red King of Helsinki: Lies, Spies and Gymnastics

ABOUT THE AUTHOR

Helena Halme grew up in Tampere, central Finland, and moved to the UK via Stockholm and Helsinki at the age of 22. She is a former BBC journalist and has also worked as a magazine editor, a bookseller and, until recently, ran a Finnish/British cultural association in London.

Since gaining an MA in Creative Writing at Bath Spa University, Helena has published 13 fiction titles, including six in *The Nordic Heart* and four in *Love on the Island* series.

Helena lives in North London with her ex-Navy husband and an old stubborn terrier, called Jerry. She loves Nordic Noir and sings along to Abba songs when no one is around.

You can read Helena's blog at www.helenahalme.-com, where you can also sign up for her *Readers' Group* and receive an exclusive, free short story, *The Day We Met*.

Find Helena Halme online
www.helenahalme.com
hello@helenahalme.com

Printed in Great Britain
by Amazon